THE WEEKEND WAS MURDER

About the author:

Joan Lowery Nixon is the author of more than ninety books for young readers, including *The Dark And Deadly Pool*, *The Other Side Of Dark* and *Shadowmaker*. She has won numerous awards for her writing, including the Edgar Allen Poe Award three times. She lives in Houston, USA with her husband.

Other titles by Joan Lowery Nixon
published by Hodder Children's Books

The Dark And Deadly Pool
The Other Side Of Dark
Shadowmaker

The Weekend Was Murder

Joan Lowery Nixon

a division of Hodder Headline plc

First published 1992 by Delacorte Press, USA

First published in Great Britain in 1993
by Hodder Children's Books
This edition published 1995

10 9 8 7 6 5 4 3 2

A Catalogue record for this book is available from the British Library.

ISBN 0 340 59622 8

Printed and bound in Great Britain by
Cox & Wyman Ltd, Reading, Berkshire

Hodder Children's Books
a division of Hodder Headline plc
338 Euston Road
London NW1 3BH

To the dedicated middle school and junior high teachers and librarians, Betty Carter, Barbara Edwards, Pam Boyd and Ken Kowan, who asked, "Will you write our kids a mystery they can act out and solve?" and to Dr Richard Abrahamson, who so generously offered his good advice.

GROUND FLOOR OF THE RIDLEY HOTEL

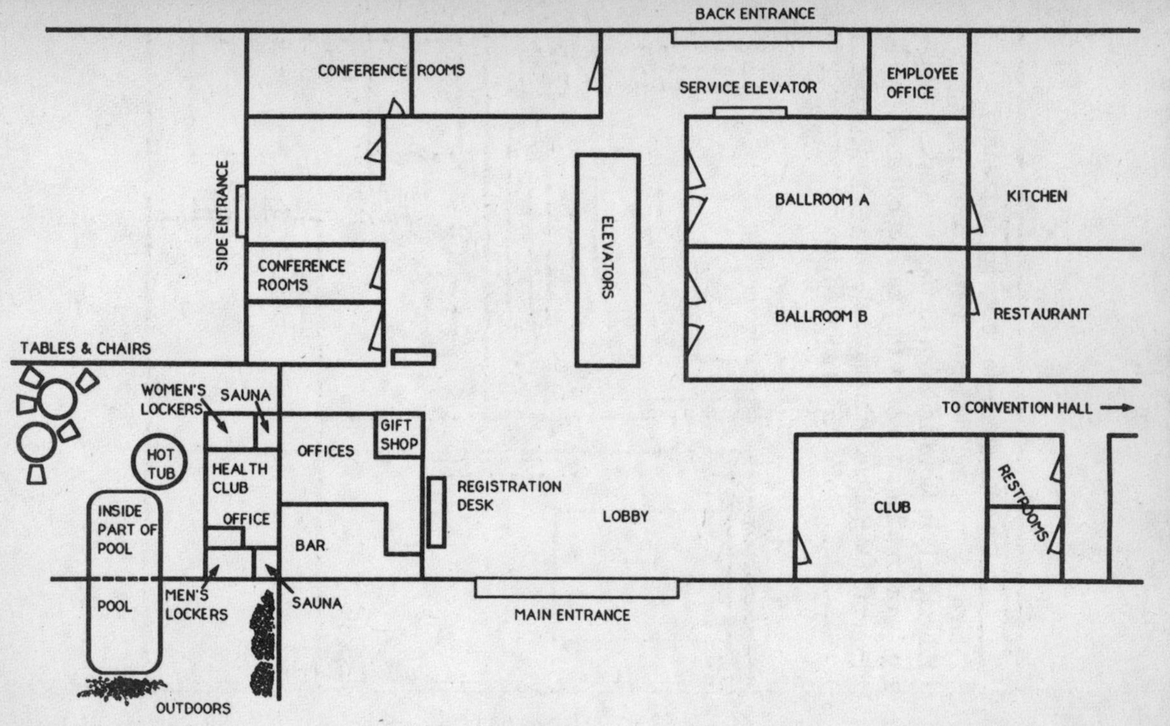

SUITE 1927

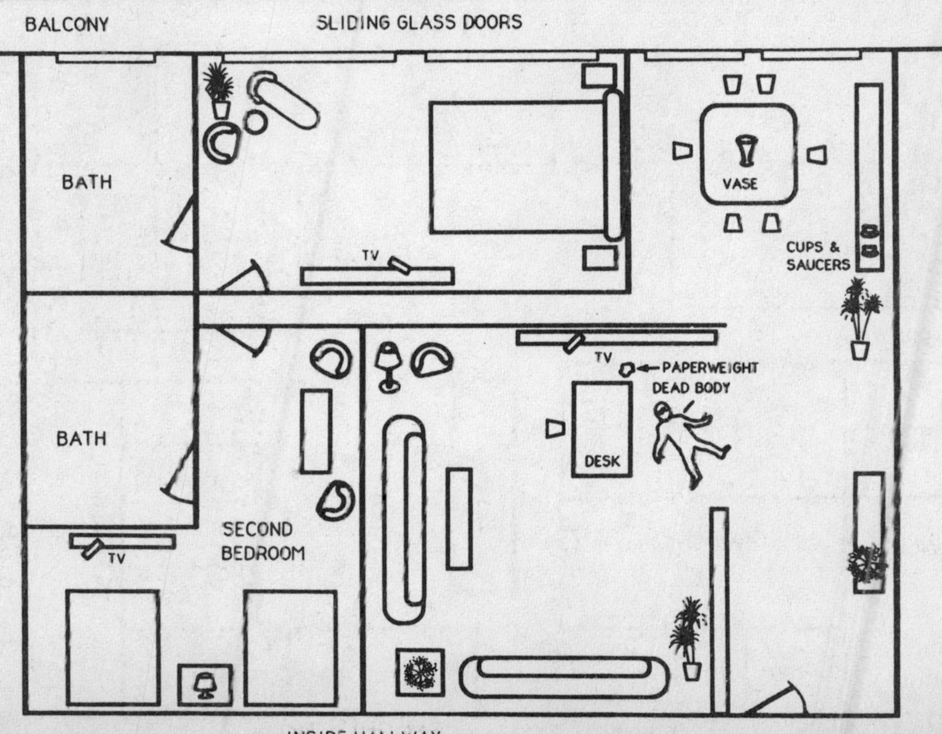

BALCONY
SLIDING GLASS DOORS
BATH
VASE
CUPS &
SAUCERS
TV
BATH
TV
PAPERWEIGHT
DEAD BODY
DESK
SECOND
BEDROOM
TV
INSIDE HALLWAY

A chilling silence filled the nineteenth floor of the Ridley Hotel as Tina Martinez and I stepped from the elevator into the hallway. Mutely lighted, the dark-paneled walls seemed to breathe inward, as though someone had suddenly stopped talking to listen intently. Tina nervously glanced to the right and the left and gave a little shiver.

"What's the matter?" I asked.

"Nothing," Tina whispered, and the whisper sounded so scary, the hair on my arms rose and began to tickle. I stared down the long, dim hallway behind us, wondering what she'd seen that I couldn't see.

Tina, who works in hotel security, tiptoed down the hall to the second door on the right. She raised a hand to knock, but stopped, turned, and stared at me with the same terrified expression on her face that I'd seen the week before when we went to a horror movie together.

"Tina, what's the matter with you?" I asked. Chills wiggled up and down my backbone.

"Never mind," she mumbled.

Never mind? What kind of an answer was that? And what was the matter with me that I'd let my imagination lead me from the beautiful Ridley Hotel into a make-believe house of horrors? I took a deep breath, threw back my shoulders, and stood as straight as I could, which is enough for most people to take notice of, since I'm five feet, ten inches tall.

Mary Elizabeth Rafferty, I told myself, *don't be a nincompoop. Even though Tina is behaving like a refugee from a Godzilla commercial, there is nothing to be afraid of here. Nothing.*

"Tina," I said in a normal voice, which seemed to boom and echo down the empty hallway, making me shudder, "this is weird. It's ten o'clock at night, I'm going off duty in the health club, and you rush in and practically beg me to come up to the nineteenth floor with you. So I do, and now you act like Frankenstein's monster is on the other side of that door. What are we doing up here, anyway?"

She struggled to get a grip on herself before she answered. "Security got another complaint about noise and loud music in room nineteen twenty-seven," she said. "Any time we get a complaint we have to check it out, and this time it was my turn."

What noise and loud music? I listened intently to the silence and looked at the number on the door to make sure we were on the right floor.

"I know," Tina said before I had a chance to ask another question. "You don't hear anything. We never do."

"Maybe whoever's staying in nineteen twenty-seven heard us coming and turned down the television."

Tina shook her head. "Nobody's staying there. The desk rarely assigns this room to a hotel guest—only when the Ridley's overbooked and someone with a reservation gets angry and starts making threats." She paused and looked nervously at the door of nineteen twenty-seven before she added, "And then we get a different kind of complaint."

"I don't get it. Complaint about what?"

"About the ghost," she said. "The Ridley tries to keep it quiet, but room nineteen twenty-seven is haunted. The maids won't set foot inside to clean unless they've got company, and the one who does bed turn-downs and leaves chocolate mints on pillows around nine o'clock each night wouldn't be caught dead inside nineteen twenty-seven when it's occupied."

I flattened myself against the wall—the opposite wall—and tried to make myself believe it wasn't holding me up. "Aw, come on," I said.

Tina, who is nineteen—three years older than I am—plans on becoming a psychiatrist someday. She's usually very levelheaded, even though she likes to point out our psychological hang-ups and offer a lot more advice than anyone wants, and this suddenly trembling excuse for a security guard didn't fit. "It's a gag, right?" I asked. "You're trying to scare me with some crazy story about ghosts."

"No, Liz. Honest, it's true," Tina insisted.

"There's really a ghost in that room? How many people have seen it?"

"No one's ever really seen it. They've just felt it, and things . . . well, peculiar things have happened."

Tina looked sincere, but I couldn't go along with this ghost thing too easily. Trying not to show how frightened I was, I asked, "Whoever heard of a psychiatrist who believes in ghosts?"

Tina didn't react the way I thought she would. Her face grew red and she got a little huffy. "Obviously, you've never heard of parapsychology and the many recorded instances of officially observed ectoplasm," she told me. "And then there's the theory of the electrically charged photographic imprint brought on by a violent death, and—"

I interrupted her. "Okay, okay. I really don't want to hear all that, so I'll just accept it. But you have to tell me, what's the story about this room?"

Tina shot a quick glance toward the door, as though she thought someone inside might be eavesdropping, and lowered her voice. "A few years ago a husband and wife stayed in this room for a week. There were some terrible arguments, and they turned up the volume on the TV and radio to try to cover them. Just ask housekeeping and room service how bad it was. Finally guests on this floor called in complaints, and Lamar himself came up to take care of things."

I could just picture the Ridley's impressive, supercool chief of security, Lamar Boudry, giving that couple his down-the-nose stare. "So that took care of that," I said. "One of Lamar's stern looks would be enough to shut anyone up in a hurry."

"It probably did, but the next day they were at it

again. The police said they must have struggled, a gun went off, and—" Tina interrupted herself. "See? It's that electrically charged photographic imprint I told you about. A violent death, and the ghost goes through it again like a cassette tape."

I envisioned a see-through woman in a filmy white nightgown who carried a lighted candle as she floated through the room. The picture may have been influenced by the last late-night movie I saw on television, but it was probably close enough.

I turned toward the elevators, eager to get as far away from that room as possible. "The ghost has turned off the noise and loud music, so let's go."

Tina grabbed my arm. "Not yet. We can't. I have to check out the room first."

Icy prickles ran up and down my back. Or were they somebody's icy fingers? "You mean go inside?" I squeaked.

Tina nodded. "That's why I brought you with me," she said. As I hung back, she pleaded, "Please, Liz. I need you. I can't do it alone."

Ever since I began my summer job in the Ridley health club, Tina had been my friend. We may not have seen eye-to-eye on everything, especially on Fran—Francis Liverpool III—because Tina thought I should hold out for a handsome boyfriend who was a lot taller than I was; and I thought Fran was the neatest, most-fun-to-be-with guy I'd ever met, and I didn't mind that he was four inches shorter than I am. That is, I didn't mind *much,* and I liked the way Fran kissed.

Tina also kept telling me, every time I dropped something or tripped over something, that my clumsiness stemmed from a lack of self-worth. Somehow she managed to tie a short boyfriend into it. I told her that I grew a lot last year, and I still wasn't used to my head being so far from my feet, but that didn't fit her pop-psychology theories. However, I liked Tina; she'd been a big help to me, and I decided I owed her a couple of favors.

"All right," I agreed, in a voice so small, it seemed to come out of my toes.

Tina nodded, raised her hand again, and knocked on the door.

I could only stare. "You knocked for a ghost? Do you expect it to open the door?"

She gave me one of those looks and said, "We have to knock before entering any of the rooms. It's a hotel rule." She pulled out her passkey and opened the door.

Reluctantly, I followed her inside, but stopped in amazement as Tina quickly flipped on a master switch. This wasn't just a room, it was a large, elegant suite. From where I stood I could see a living room with deep sofas, glass tables, and a carved desk with gleaming bronze bookends, pencil holder, and paperweight. Beyond was a dining area, with a glass wall opening onto a balcony, and between the living room and dining room was a short hallway that probably led to a bedroom and bath. Everything was white and gold, soft and plush, mirrored and sparkly, with just a few accents of pale blue. A small crystal chandelier hung in the entryway over our heads, and a large one graced the dining room.

It didn't look like the kind of creepy, cobwebby place where a ghost would hang out, and there were no cold chills or floating, staring eyes. I was so fascinated with the suite, I didn't even think about ghosts.

And I couldn't resist looking into the nearest mirror, which framed the room behind me. "Wow!" I said. "This place was designed for a redhead. All I'd need is the right designer gown to go with it."

"And a ton of money to pay the bill," Tina said. "Don't touch anything. You know how you are," she admonished, and began to walk through the living room.

I followed, chattering away. I picked up the paperweight, which was heavy enough to be real bronze, steadied the tall blown-glass vase that rocked a little as I gently brushed the table, and examined the delicate white-and-gold china demitasse cups on a sideboard in the dining area. I lifted one to examine it, but Tina froze, so I put it down again, managing to catch it before it rolled off the edge. I knew I was klutzy. I didn't need Tina to remind me.

"This is fantastic! I didn't even dream the Ridley had a suite like this," I said.

"There are five of them on this floor—all of them on this north side," Tina told me, "but only two are occupied right now—the one at the end of the hall and the one next to that."

"I don't get it. The people way down there couldn't hear noise coming from this suite," I said.

"The one at the end did," Tina told me. Then, as though she suspected someone of hiding there, she carefully opened each of the cupboards under the built-in bar, which was in a waist-high divider that stood in front of the hallway entrance between the left side of the living room and the dining room. Tina went on to explain, "He's a businessman from Japan, here for a meeting with some financial-investment group—that one Mr. Parmegan is in on. Rita, in housekeeping, says the man's a candy-bar freak. The guy in the suite next to his is in that financial group too. I wonder if . . ."

I wasn't interested in a financial group, especially if it had any connection to the manager of the Ridley, who was a gracious host to hotel guests but about as friendly as Oscar the Grouch to his employees.

"What about the other suites?" I asked. "The hotel's giving me a room during the weekend because I'm one of the staff who'll have to give out clues when they put on that murder-mystery weekend. Do you think there's any chance that . . ."

"None," Tina said. She stopped and turned to look at me. I could see that she had something on her mind, and I wondered if she'd tell me about it. Tina loves good gossip. But she just said, "By tonight all the rest of the suites will be occupied."

"Has there ever been a murder-mystery weekend at the Ridley before?" I asked.

"No," she said. "It's something new here, which is probably why they sold out right away. There's a limit. Only one hundred and fifty people can play the game."

I shrugged. "It doesn't seem like much of a game to me. I don't know why people would want to pretend to solve a crime."

"Laura . . . You know Laura Dale, don't you?"

"Of course I know Laura. She's head of the Ridley's public relations. She's the one who got the idea to put on this mystery thing."

"Okay, then," Tina went on. "Laura told me it's like being inside a mystery novel. People who love to read mysteries want to see if they can solve one, too, given the chance."

One hundred and fifty supersleuths running around the hotel? This was going to be something to see.

Tina thought a moment, then seemed to make up her mind. She pulled out a chair from the dining table and sat down, motioning to me to do the same. Her eyes glittered and she lowered her voice as she said, "Liz, this is top secret, but I'll trust you not to tell anyone. There's something even more exciting than a mystery weekend going on at the Ridley. You know that big stolen-securities–money-laundering trial that's going to begin on Monday?"

"No," I said.

She was so surprised that for a moment she seemed to lose her train of thought. "What do you mean, 'no'? Aren't you interested in local crime news?"

"I try to avoid it."

"Hmmm. Obviously an infantile return-to-the-womb response," she said. "For your own welfare you should—"

I interrupted. "What about the trial?"

Tina remembered what she'd been talking about, and her enthusiasm returned. "Well! The district attorney's key witness is a secretary who knows how the guy on trial managed it and can identify some of the syndicate people he dealt with. Lamar said her testimony's so important, it could bring about the conviction. The only problem is that a prowler, who may or may not have anything to do with the syndicate, was chased away from the apartment complex where she lives, and now she's terrified that her life is in danger, so she's going to be sequestered with a policewoman here at the Ridley."

Tina proudly squared her shoulders, and her uniform of white shirt and maroon jacket and slacks looked even better filled out than usual. "Of course, Lamar and I and the rest of our security staff will be helping to protect her."

"Why did the desk put her up here in a suite?"

"The suites have got two bedrooms," she answered, "one for the witness and one for the policewoman."

I counted on my fingers. "There's still one more suite. If it's going to be empty . . ."

"Don't get your hopes up," she said. "The one on the other side of this suite will be occupied by that mystery writer and her daughter, the actress, who are putting on the mystery weekend."

"Yikes!" I said. "Do mystery writers make *that* much money?"

"Not on your life," she said. "For them it's a comp."

"Which means?"

"Complimentary. The hotel's paying for it."

There was a loud buzz on Tina's walkie-talkie, which made us both jump. It was Lamar, of course, and Tina convinced him she was simply doing a thorough checkup.

She hooked the walkie-talkie back on her belt, said, "Come on," to me, and walked into the first bedroom. I was right behind her, and when I saw that room I made a little strangling noise of total admiration and naked jealousy.

Filmy gauze swooped from a gilded crown to frame the gigantic bed with its rose velvet spread, and I am probably exaggerating a bit, but the soft, white carpet had to be close to knee-deep. The outside wall was glass, and I pulled back the sheer curtains to see another sliding glass door leading to a balcony that ran across that side of the hotel. It was perfect, except for the view. All I could see was the tops of nearby buildings, and I couldn't imagine why anyone would go out on the balcony when the view inside the room was so much better.

Tina unplugged both the clock radio next to the bed and the television set in the armoire. "Just in case one of these was turned on by mistake," she told me, although she knew as well as I did that with no one in the room there was no way it could happen. I began to feel creepy again.

She did a fast tour of the second bedroom—which was pretty, but not movie-star pretty like the first—and the gigantic marble bathroom. I stayed right behind her. What impressed me most was the telephone in the bathroom. Imagine! In the bathroom! As though there wasn't a telephone in every room of that suite.

Tina winced and jumped back as she jerked open the closed shower curtain. When nobody lunged out at us, she let go of my arm, gave a huge sigh of relief and said, "Okay, it's done. Let's get out of here."

But as we left the bedroom area a strange thing happened. The air seemed to grow colder and riffle against the back of my neck. "Maybe we should adjust the air-conditioning in here. It's awfully cold," I said, as I gave a quick glance toward Tina.

Tina didn't answer, and her face told me something I didn't want to know. She broke into a run, but I beat her time by at least three seconds and might have been faster if I hadn't tripped over a small footstool and gone sprawling.

"Hurry up!" Tina said. She had the front door open by the time I scrambled to my feet. And as she turned off the light switch I thought I heard her murmur, "Don't leave me."

"I'm not going to leave you," I said.

At the same time she said to me, "What is that supposed to mean? I'm not going to leave you."

I gasped and stammered, "Y-you said it. I didn't."

"No, I didn't. You did."

"I did not!"

We stared, wide-eyed, as it dawned on us who had spoken. Then we screeched and slammed against each other as we raced out the door, bouncing off the walls in our mad dash for the elevator. As though we were little kids, we jabbed at the button over and over and hopped up and down, whimpering and squeaking.

Suddenly the elevator doors slid open, a headless man in a tuxedo thrust himself toward me, and I screamed.

"Sorry," the bellman named Ziggy said. "I didn't know anybody would be standing there." He pulled back his luggage cart, on the end of which stood a fully clothed dressmaker's dummy, and swung it sideways, passing around me.

"I do like that scream," a woman trilled. She followed Ziggy out of the elevator and beamed at Tina and me. "Now, which one of you darling girls made that beautifully loud noise?"

"She did," Tina answered quickly. "I'm with security."

I recognized the woman immediately as Roberta Kingston Duffy, the mystery writer. I'd met her when she'd visited the Ridley Hotel a couple of months ago, getting acquainted with the layout before she wrote the script for the murder-mystery weekend. Mrs. Duffy had short, curly gray hair, a round, rosy-cheeked face, and reminded me of my grandmother. But my grandmother behaves in a normal way and doesn't carry dressmaker's dummies in tuxedos around with her, or compliment people on their screams, or sit in the coffee shop making notes and mumbling aloud about whether her current victim should be shot, stabbed, or poisoned.

A much younger woman, Mrs. Duffy's daughter, Eileen, stepped out of the elevator and joined us. She was my height, and her hair was as red as mine. The only difference was that someone might think about me, "Liz has such a sweet face," whereas anyone who looked at Eileen Duffy would immediately think, "Wow!" and try to remember if they'd seen her on the cover of *Vogue* or in a current movie.

Mrs. Duffy began to introduce herself and her daughter, but I said, "We met you on your first trip to the Ridley, and I've read all of your really great mystery novels, but I don't expect you to remember us. This is Tina Martinez, and I'm Liz Rafferty. Tina works in security, and I've got a summer job here in the—"

Mrs. Duffy held up a hand to stop me. "Don't tell me," she said. "I love to play detective, so I'm going to guess." She then studied me from top to toe as she said, "Your hair has curled in little ringlets around your face, which shows you've recently been in an area that's probably warm and damp. Your tennis shoes are almost spotless, although they're slightly run down on the inside of both heels, which means that although you've owned them for a month or so, you've always worn them indoors. You're wearing shorts, so I'll say that you work in the Ridley health club and you've recently come off duty. Am I right?"

"Yes!" Tina exclaimed. "That's fantastic."

It wasn't bad, but Mrs. Duffy could have reached the same conclusion if she'd just read the words, RIDLEY HEALTH CLUB, that were printed in large letters on the front of my pink T-shirt.

Eileen grinned at me as though we were in on a secret. "I remember you, Liz," she said. "You're my witness in the health club. Did you get the information sheet that lists what you're supposed to tell the people playing the mystery if they question you?"

I nodded. "I've gone over the material and practiced being questioned, so I don't think I'll make any mistakes."

"Of course you won't, dear," Mrs. Duffy said, and turned to her daughter. "Don't you think we should give Mary Elizabeth an additional job? She'd make a great screamer."

"It's fine with me," Eileen said. "Liz can have the job if she wants it."

I didn't understand what they were talking about. "I'm supposed to scream? Where? When?"

Eileen answered, "During Friday evening's party someone has to run into the room screaming loudly, practically collapse in the chief of security's arms, and tell us that she's found a body."

"Thank you very much," I blurted out, "but I did find a body once, and I'd rather not do it again." As I pictured that horrible Mr. Kamara floating facedown in the Ridley swimming pool, I shuddered.

"Really? You found a real body?" Mrs. Duffy asked, and her eyes lit up. "I'd love to hear all about it. You must tell me—"

Before she could continue, her daughter stepped in. "There's nothing to worry about, Liz," Eileen said. "Our script is all fun and make-believe. We use professional actors as the suspects, I play the part of the detective, and there won't be a real body. We'll just draw an outline on the carpet around one of our actors with masking tape. It will be on the floor at the scene of the crime along with clues we'll put here and there, and we won't let the participants examine the crime scene until after we read them the coroner's and the crime lab's reports on Saturday morning."

"The coroner and the crime lab sound real," I told her.

"We have to be realistic as far as the plot and the clues are concerned," Eileen said. "We have to play fair, so every clue must be there." She waited a moment and asked, "Well? What's your answer?"

Why shouldn't I do it? It beat scrubbing tiles in the health club. I'd be glad to leave that job to Deely Johnson, our new health-club director. "All right," I answered, but a question occurred to me. "Where is the scene of the crime?"

Mrs. Duffy smiled. "We've got a good one," she answered, "a whole suite in which to plant clues. As a matter of fact, it's on this very floor—room nineteen twenty-seven."

I spoke without thinking. "Oh, no! That suite is haunted!"

"Your public relations manager told us," she said. "That's why the suite is available for our crime scene."

"But the ghost—"

"My dear Mary Elizabeth," Mrs. Duffy said, "I don't believe in ghosts."

It was hard to keep my mouth from falling open and staying there. "But you write about ghosts. There are ghosts in some of your mystery novels," I insisted.

"I invent them and write about them because people love to be frightened," she said. "My ghosts are no more real than the ghost in that silly story about room nineteen twenty-seven."

It was obvious that the two of us did not look at life the same way. I gulped and squeaked, "I really don't think I want to be your screamer."

"Oh, you don't have to come up here," Mrs. Duffy explained. "We'll just want you to race out of the elevator and run screaming into the ballroom next door. You don't have to take the elevator any higher than the second floor."

I gave a huge sigh of relief. "Then it's okay. I'll take the job," I said.

Ziggy had put their bags into room nineteen twenty-five, next to the haunted room, and was coughing quietly to himself, hoping he could get his tip and leave.

"Mom," Eileen said, "the bellman's waiting, and it's late. We've got to make sure our actors are settled in and get them together for a run-through. I want to take the whole thing from the top."

But Mrs. Duffy said, "I'd love to hear about this body Liz found."

"Later," Eileen told her, and said to us, before she pulled her mother away, "We'll see you tomorrow afternoon at rehearsal."

The moment we got on the elevator, Tina grabbed my arm and cried, "Liz! She may write a book about how you found Mr. Kamara's body floating in the swimming pool and how you helped solve the thefts at the Ridley! You could be famous!"

I just shrugged and tried to look modest. What could I say? I was thinking the same thing myself.

"It would have to have a scary title," Tina went on. "Something like *Horror Night at the Ridley* or *Thieves Who Sneak Through the Darkness*."

I looked at her and said, "Yuck."

"Let's see. The murder took place in the dark in the swimming pool." Her eyes narrowed and her forehead scrunched into little wrinkles as she worked on it. "Never mind," she said. "I'll come up with something."

The next morning as I packed my suitcase, Mom came into my room, sat on the bed, and said, "Aren't you going to have fun!"

That haunted room had interfered with my sleep, and I couldn't get it out of my mind. "I don't think so," I told her.

"Of course you are. Your aunt Sally went to one of those mystery weekends and said it was a fantastic experience. Teams were all over the place trying to find clues and solve the crime. The competition grew fierce. A woman was pushed into the swimming pool, and a man swore he was being followed. It was great fun."

"A laugh riot," I said, and folded the last of my pink health-club T-shirts. Since my instructions said that I'd have to be easily identifiable at all times in uniform, those regulation shirts, white shorts, white socks, and tennies were as dressy as I'd get. I didn't have much of a wardrobe problem.

I tossed in my makeup, hairbrush, and comb, snapped the case shut, and tried to catch it before it fell off the end of the bed. I didn't make it. It bounced against my shins, so I sat down beside Mom to rub my aching legs and asked, "What kind of people come to these mystery-weekend things?"

"People who love to read mysteries," she said. "They've read so many they think they can solve them."

"Like being a cop?"

"More like being an amateur detective character, like those in some of the mysteries they've read."

"That's just what Tina told me, but it seems like an awful lot of work. You'd have to think hard all weekend."

"The people who participate are intelligent people. They like to use their minds."

Mom gave me one of those knowing looks, and I knew that the next thing she was going to do was suggest I follow their good example, so I said, "If those people were still in high school, they'd use their minds. Boy, would they use their minds! If they had Mrs. Barclay for civics, they'd never stop using their minds. When I graduate from high school, I'm going to give my mind a vacation. For at least one week I'm not going to think about anything."

"Very funny," Mom said. But I wasn't being funny.

I slumped and stared at my shoes. "It's going to be a long weekend," I said. "I just wish that Fran had been chosen to be one of the staff witnesses. This is his weekend off duty, and I can't share it with him." It was also the last day of July, with little more than three weeks left before my job would be over and the fall semester would begin. I was going to miss working at the Ridley.

"So that's why you aren't looking forward to the mystery weekend—because Fran won't be there." Mom smiled and squeezed my shoulders, and I guess she understood how I felt, but I didn't want to admit anything. After all, she was my mother.

Just then the doorbell rang. Mom hopped to her feet, I dragged myself to mine, and we both headed toward the door. Hopping beats dragging, so she got there first.

Fran burst in. His hair was tousled and his cowlick was sticking up, but he grinned at me and shouted, "Liz! I just got a call from my boss in room service! With all that's going on at the Ridley this weekend, they need everyone in room service to stay on duty, and because it's my weekend off, they want me to be a witness in my room-service uniform for the mystery weekend!"

"Great!" I yelled. Immediately the weekend began to look interesting.

Mom straightened the pictures that had bounced out of place when one of my outflung arms accidentally hit the wall, and Fran said, "I've got a neat part. I'm going to narrow my eyes and say things like, 'The woman who was dressed head to foot in black called room service for coffee, and when I saw the packet of poison in her hand I knew immediately that she had evil intentions.' "

"That's awful!" I said. "I've read Mrs. Duffy's books. She's a good writer, so I know she didn't write that!"

"I just made it up," Fran admitted. "I won't get my instruction sheet until I get to the hotel." He looked a little hurt. "It wasn't that bad, was it?"

"It was too melodramatic," I told him. "Our instructions say that we're supposed to act natural and normal. We're just hotel employees who happen to have heard or seen some things that might be clues."

"We'll see." Fran gave a wicked chuckle and pretended to twirl a long mustache.

"You're impossible," I said, and ran to get my shoulder bag and suitcase.

It was hard to say a quick good-bye to Mom, because at the door she held my shoulders, peered into my face as though I were on my way to Alaska, and asked, "They will feed you, won't they?"

"Of course, Mom," I said. "We'll eat all our meals in the employees' cafeteria."

"Remember, Mary Elizabeth, to choose a green vegetable and a salad with your entree, and no junk food."

"Mom, you know I *live* for junk food," I said.

"Very funny," she said again, but I still wasn't trying to be funny.

I kissed her good-bye, then ran after Dad and his lawn mower to kiss him good-bye too.

Dad, who was sweaty and blotchy with little grass and dirt specks all over his bare chest, turned off the motor so that we could hear each other. "Liz," he said, "your aunt Sally assured us that there were no elements of danger or daring in this mystery thing, that it's all in fun."

"That's what the author told me."

"Good," he said. "Did she tell you exactly what you'll have to do?"

I nodded. "If anybody asks me, I have to tell them about an argument I overheard in the health club between two of the suspects. But first of all I have to run in, screaming that I've found a body."

He gave a start of surprise, then relaxed as he studied my face. "Good. If you can make light of your experience, then I guess that means you're beginning to handle things now."

"No more nightmares about Mr. Kamara," I said, and managed to smile.

"Have a good time, sweetheart," Dad told me, and went back to mowing the grass.

I didn't want Dad or Mom to worry, so I kept to myself the memories of finding Mr. Kamara's body floating in the hotel's swimming pool. Never, I promised myself. Never, ever, did I want to discover another dead body!

I threw my things into the backseat of Fran's old car, which he calls Yellow Belly, and we headed for the hotel.

On the way I told him about the haunted room, but he just said, "Didn't you know that? I knew that," which was infuriating.

I asked, "Were you ever inside the room?"

"No," he admitted, so it was my turn to be smug.

"Well, I was," I said, "and the ghost even talked to me—to Tina and me, that is."

Fran took his eyes off the road for a quick glance in my direction. "The ghost talked? What did it say?"

"Tina had just turned off the lights, when the ghost said, 'Don't leave me.' "

Fran laughed so hard, I was glad we were stopped at a red light. "Some ghost," he finally managed to say. "Was he scared with the lights out?"

I changed the subject, because there'd be no convincing Fran. I knew what I'd heard, and I remembered only too clearly how scared Tina and I had been. I never wanted to set foot in that haunted room again.

We parked in the employees' section at the far end of the lot behind the hotel. I fully intended to emerge as gracefully as possible from the Yellow Belly, but tripped over the door frame and landed on my hands and knees. As Fran helped me up, I thought how glad I was that Tina wasn't there, and uncomfortably, I wondered if she might be right. Maybe the way I felt about myself *did* have something to do with my short boyfriend and my clumsiness.

Fran and I walked toward the back door, arriving just behind a middle-aged woman who was in the clutches of a tall, uniformed policewoman on one side and Lamar Boudry on the other. The woman wasn't dowdy, just sort of dumpy. Her dark-brown hair was pulled back tightly and fastened in a lump. Her eyes and face were pale, and the severe, navy-blue suit she wore did nothing for her.

Even though their pace was a brisk one, Lamar and the policewoman snapped their heads from one side to the other as they kept a sharp eye on the parking lot. Now and then the woman twisted to throw nervous glances over her shoulder, and when she saw Fran and me coming up behind them she stiffened and gave a little moan.

Lamar and the policewoman had such a firm grip on her upper arms that she didn't cause them to miss a step, but they both turned to stare at us.

"Hotel employees," I heard Lamar say as they continued on their way.

"Somebody's under arrest," Fran whispered to me.

"No," I whispered back. I stopped, letting Lamar and the women with him enter the hotel, so I could fill Fran in. "Do you know about the stolen-securities-money-laundering trial that's going to start in Houston on Monday?"

"Sure," he said. "Doesn't everybody?"

I didn't bother to answer that one. I just repeated what Tina had told me about the sequestered witness who thought her life was in danger. "But don't tell anybody," I cautioned.

We cut through the back hallway, passing the service elevator, where Lamar was waiting with the policewoman and the witness. Just then a door to one of the small conference rooms opened, and Eileen Duffy and a group of people—probably her actors—filed out. I saw the witness nervously cling to the policewoman as she studied each face, then suddenly relax when none of them were recognizable to her. The actors went on their way, following Eileen, and I walked with Fran in the direction of the lobby and the registration desk. That witness was one scared woman, and I felt sorry for her. Maybe when she was sequestered in one of those beautiful suites on the nineteenth floor she'd be able to relax and feel more secure.

Although it was early afternoon the lobby was filled with people and there were lines at the registration desk, but some of the people in those lines didn't look like anyone I'd ever seen at the Ridley before. A tall man, who was wearing a deerstalker hat and had that Sherlock Holmes kind of curved pipe in his mouth, was staring at the woman in front of him through a magnifying glass. A young woman swathed in a long, black cape swept past me, and two elderly women in red and black T-shirts from Houston's mystery bookstore, Murder by the Book, swiveled in place, studying everyone in the room with deep suspicion.

When the glance of the shorter of the two fell upon me, her intense gaze was replaced by a pleased grin, and the woman shouted, "Yoo-hoo! Mary Elizabeth! Over here!"

I smiled back and went to greet Mrs. Sylvia Bandini and her best friend, Mrs. Opal Larabee, two of the health club's regulars.

"We were the first to sign up," Mrs. Bandini said.

"We're naturals," Mrs. Larabee chimed in, so excited that she reminded me of a fat little bird, hopping on a tree limb. "Look what a good job we did in finding out who killed Mr. Kamara."

Mrs. Bandini had the grace to look embarrassed. "Opal," she said, "Detective Jarvis told us we were the best eyewitnesses he had ever met, but *we* didn't find out who killed Mr. Kamara. Mary Elizabeth did."

"Oh," Mrs. Larabee said. "Well, I would greatly appreciate it if you wouldn't bring that subject up around my house, since my grandchildren happen to have a different impression."

"If you can't be honest with your grandchildren, who can you be honest with?"

"Can I help it if they jumped to conclusions?"

"Maybe you'll solve *this* mystery," I told them, and hurried to join Fran at the end of the reception desk.

One of the clerks nodded to us and handed us our room keys.

Mrs. Duffy was standing close by, reading the list of people who had registered for the murder-mystery weekend, and I heard her saying to Laura Dale, who had a copy of the list, "It's my fault. I told you to limit the number to one hundred and fifty, but there's always a last-minute cancellation or two, and I should have given you the opportunity to compile a short waiting list."

"I'm sure they'll all be here," Laura said. "We were sold out just a day or two after the ad appeared."

"Come on," Fran said to me. "I'm on the fourth floor. Where's your room? I'll go up with you first."

I looked at the number on the key. "Fifth," I said. I was kind of excited about this weekend, in spite of my earlier misgivings. I'd be playing a role, I'd be part of the fun, and I felt very sophisticated about having my own hotel room.

If I didn't already know how low the Ridley manager, Mr. Lewis Parmegan, rated his employees, I would have figured it out when I stepped inside my room. Someone had thoughtfully decorated a broom closet in a flowered blue print. There was barely enough room for the bed and a small dresser. The bathroom was teeny-tiny, and the view from the window consisted of the trash bins and part of a brick wall.

As I tossed my suitcase on the bed Fran said, "Uh-oh. According to the number on my room key, I'm right below you. I bet I get the same spacious accommodations."

"Oh, who cares?" I said. "We won't be in our rooms very much anyway. Why don't we go down to the coffee shop and get a soft drink?"

"Great idea!" Fran said. He waited until I'd tucked my key into one of the pockets in my shorts, and we went down to Fran's room on the fourth floor. It was a duplicate of my room, only in green.

The visit to the coffee shop was a dismal failure too, because we'd no sooner seated ourselves in one of the booths than the waitress hissed at us, "What are you doing in here? You know employees aren't allowed in the restaurants while they're in uniform!"

I felt as though everyone was staring at us as we squeezed out of the booth, but Fran took my hand and guided me down the side hallway, which led to a number of meeting rooms. In some of them we could hear people talking into crackling microphones, and Fran passed those rooms by. He stopped at the doors of two rooms, looked inside, then went on. But when Fran poked his head into a small, wood-paneled conference room, he popped out again and smiled. "Here's what I was looking for," he said. "It's empty, and no one's picked up the leftovers. Hey, Liz! There's a whole plate of cookies!"

The room held only a large, oval conference table and chairs, and—against the wall—a serving table with one of those pleated cloths that snaps on three sides and hangs to the floor. On the table were a coffee urn and cups, iced soft drinks, and a tray of assorted cookies. A few of the cups had been used and were still on the conference table, along with some rumpled candy-bar wrappers.

"It's all right to eat the cookies. They'll just throw them out," Fran said. But he had no sooner stuffed one into his mouth than we heard the door handle turn. With one mind we dove under the serving table.

I sat there shaking and clutching the can of cola I'd just opened, thankful that the pleated cloth went all the way down to the floor, hiding us from whoever had come into the room. What had we done? Surely we'd be fired if anyone found us under here.

A deep voice spoke as the door shut. "The meeting went very well," he said. "We've got them where we want them."

I was almost ready to crawl out and beg for mercy, when the other voice answered, "You'd better be right. It could be your last chance. I only hope you've got those papers in order—"

The first man interrupted. "We've discussed it enough, Al. Don't bring it up again. We can't risk being overheard."

"Don't worry," Al said. "For the last few years I've worked closely with you on all your projects. You should know by this time that I'm not going to let anyone get in our way."

"Including me?"

"What are you talking about?"

When the other man didn't answer, Al said, "Frank, we're partners. You have no reason not to trust me."

There was another pause, and the man called Frank said, "There's something else we need to talk about.

I'm a little concerned about Mr. Yamoto. He's an intelligent man and very cautious."

"Which is probably why he got to be as rich as he did."

"I get the feeling he's going to double-check everything I tell him."

"You mean with a private investigator? Let him. We're covered." Al chuckled and said, "Frank, you can see it. Yamoto is as eager to get in on a good thing as anyone else. The idea of getting something for nothing—he won't be able to resist it. Logan too. He's hooked, thanks to Parmegan."

Fran and I stared at each other. Were they talking about Lewis Parmegan, the manager of the Ridley?

"You catch big fish if you've got the right bait," Frank said. "I had a hunch Parmegan would make good bait."

There was some moving about, and Al asked, "How about another cup of coffee?"

I could hear them approaching, and one of them stood so close to the table I could see the tips of his shoes under the cloth. I tried to shrink back and not breathe so they wouldn't discover us, but I dropped my soft-drink can, and it gushed out, all over the toes of the man's shoes, as it spread from under the table and across the carpet.

We heard the door open, and the shoes whipped around in that direction. Someone said, "Oh, sorry, sir. I thought this room had been vacated."

"It's all right. You can pick up the dishes. We were just leaving," Al answered.

There was the sound of coffee cups being put down over our heads, footsteps moving away from our direction, and the door shutting. But a voice so close that it made me jump grumbled, "What a mess! Some nerd spilled his drink, but I'm the one who has to clean it up."

I was a nerd, all right, to be so clumsy. How could I have done that?

He muttered some opinions that weren't very nice, and I squeezed my eyes shut and stopped breathing as I waited to be discovered. To my surprise I heard the muttering trickle toward the door.

"He's going to get some wet towels to mop it up," Fran whispered.

As the door shut again Fran and I scrambled out from under that table. Fran snatched up a few more cookies, and we made a dash from the conference room into the hall.

It wasn't until we were out of danger of being caught that I dared to ask Fran, "What was all that about Mr. Parmegan?"

Fran looked uncomfortable. "It sounded like some kind of a con game, with Mr. Parmegan involved in it."

"Sometimes Mr. Parmegan can be a real hard nose," I said.

"A mean machine."

"A jerk head. But I don't think he'd willingly try to cheat anyone, do you?"

"No," Fran said. "I don't."

"Should we tell Mr. Parmegan what we heard?"

"How can we?" Fran asked. "We don't know who was talking. We don't even know what the men look like."

I saw Mr. Parmegan just up ahead, and I tugged at Fran's arm. "There he is," I said. "We can at least tell him what the men said about him."

Fran's eyes grew big. "You want to tell Mr. Parmegan that somebody thinks he makes good bait?"

I stood very still. "Uh . . . why don't *you* tell him?"

"First of all, why don't we find out more about all this?" Fran suggested. "When we've got some real information, we can lay it all out and maybe skip the part about the bait."

"You're wonderful," I said. "I like the way you think."

"I have many other good qualities too," Fran said with a grin.

"I know," I murmured and moved a little closer.

But Mr. Parmegan—who looked like a successful hotel manager in his expensive dark-blue suit and color-coordinated tie—had spotted us. He stepped up beside us and said, "I believe you both are employee-witnesses for this mystery program, are you not?"

"Yes," I said, and Fran nodded agreement.

Mr. Parmegan looked at his watch. "Very well, then. You have approximately two minutes and twenty-three seconds to reach the rehearsal meeting Miss Duffy has scheduled in conference room C. It is important to be on time."

"Yes, sir," Fran said. We picked up the pace and hurried back toward the conference rooms. We were no sooner out of Mr. Parmegan's earshot than Fran muttered, "Shows how much he knows. We had two minutes and *forty-eight* seconds." We entered room C, which had been set up with chairs in an oval around the small room, and took places near the door. A few other employees had arrived, some of them chatting with the actors, but the meeting hadn't been called to order yet.

Eileen Duffy, her kelly-green dress floating behind her, sailed into the room and immediately took charge. She smiled at the members of the hotel staff who were playing witnesses—Phyllis, from the front desk; Earl from accounting, who was subbing for a doorman because the hotel couldn't spare the real doorman; Judy, the concierge; Ella from housekeeping; Fran and me.

After introducing us to the actors, she invited us to sit

down, then called her actors together and explained their roles.

"We are members of a touring theatrical company, The Pitts Players, which is directed by Hollywood impresario Edgar Albert Pitts. Our motto is, 'For Theater Hits, We're the Pitts.' "

She waited until everyone had finished giggling, then introduced the actors. "I'm not going to tell you their real names at this time," she said, "because they're going to remain in character during the entire evening, and I want you to think of them only by their character names."

She motioned to a beautiful blond woman, who was probably in her mid-twenties. "This is Crystal Crane," she said. "Crystal has talent, so she'll have a great opportunity in theater, if only she can get out of her contract with Edgar Pitts."

Crystal stepped back, and a tall, bald, middle-aged man with a big grin stepped forward. "This is Randolph Hamilton," Eileen began, but stopped. "Where's your mustache and wig?" she asked him.

"I brought it," he said. "Do I have to start wearing it now?"

"Of course. We want everyone to see you the way you'll look throughout the mystery. Put it on, please, while I introduce Annabelle Maloney."

Randolph went to a far chair and bent to rummage in a small case. We stopped watching him when a thin, mousy woman stepped up. She gazed at us shyly, blushed, and ducked her head.

"Oh, that's great, Annabelle." Eileen gave her a pat

on the shoulder and said to us, "As you can see, Annabelle is totally intimidated by Mr. Pitts. She not only plays bit parts, she also serves as his secretary and bookkeeper." She turned toward the group of actors again, saying, "And now—"

But Randolph Hamilton stepped forward. "Okay now?" he asked.

I was amazed. He looked like a different person. His dark-brown hair was stylishly cut, and his mustache was trim and handsome. He had suddenly turned into a man who looked both successful and sophisticated. Randolph held his head a little higher, and even the way he moved his body was different.

Phyllis, the desk clerk who was seated next to me, murmured aloud to herself, "I've seen him before. Where have I seen him?"

Eileen beamed at Randolph. "Marvelous," she said. "You're very much the sophisticated actor." She winked at us and said, "Randolph has the good looks, but not much talent, which is why his career lately is on the skids. It might help Randolph if he could only remember his lines!"

With a haughty toss of his shoulders, which made Annabelle giggle, Randolph stepped back, and a short man stumbled forward. He wrung his hands nervously as he stared at our small audience.

"This is Arthur Butler, one of the Pitts Players actors," Eileen said.

"Butler? I know! The butler did it," Fran said.

Eileen smiled. "Did he? It's up to our participants to figure that one out."

"I think he's a red herring," I said. I like to read mystery novels, so I know all about red herrings and things like that, which mystery authors use to confuse readers.

"Don't be too sure," Eileen said. "All I can tell you is that Arthur is a frustrated actor, because he would rather write plays than act in them."

She held out a hand to a man who was probably in his late twenties. He leisurely strolled to join her, and his glance at the rest of us was both amused and slightly contemptuous.

"The last character I want you to meet is Martin Jones," Eileen said. "He's Edgar Pitts's nephew. A little spoiled, a little sneaky, and a compulsive gambler."

"He has to be the murderer," Phyllis said.

"Who really is the murderer?" Earl asked Eileen.

"Look at their eyes," Ella said. "The murderer may give himself away."

Eileen smiled. "The actors don't always know which one of them committed the murder until our rehearsal the night before the arrest scene takes place. Mom rearranges all her scripts so that the crucial clue changes, and that changes the identity of the murderer."

She looked at each of the witnesses. "Are there any more questions?"

"Yes," I said. "You haven't introduced us to everybody. Where's Edgar Albert Pitts?"

"Edgar Albert Pitts will not be making an appearance, Liz," Eileen said. "It's his body you're going to find."

I blushed, and everyone laughed except Fran, who—

without a word—took my hand snugly into his. That was another neat thing about Fran. He understood when I needed someone to hang on to.

Eileen began to give instructions to each of the hotel employees who were going to be witnesses. "Don't make up information or add anything," she cautioned. "Keep remembering, we don't want to lead the participants astray, so all the clues have to be honest. If one of the players asks you something you don't know, just answer, 'I don't know.' You each have something to tell them—an argument you've overheard, something you've seen." She nodded to Phyllis. "You've got a list of exactly what times each of our characters checked into the hotel. Just give them that information when they ask."

"There's something else typed on my sheet," Phyllis said. She looked down at the paper in her hand and back at Eileen. "Randolph Hamilton demanded a suite, but we couldn't give it to him. Then he demanded a deluxe room, but I couldn't help him there either."

"I hope he didn't end up with a room like ours," I murmured to Fran, and he grinned back.

"Right," Eileen said. She fished into an oversized handbag and pulled out a sheet of paper, which she gave to Fran. "Sorry you got your instructions a little late," she said. "As you can see, you delivered breakfast to Annabelle Maloney and interrupted an argument between her and Crystal Crane, who was dressed to go out and who had just stopped by to talk to Annabelle."

"About what?" Fran asked.

"What does it say on your sheet? Take it from the top."

Fran read, "Miss Maloney had been crying, because her eyes were all red, and I heard Miss Crane say, 'You'll be in trouble if they find out.' " He raised his head and looked at Eileen. "Find out what?"

"That's for the people at our mystery weekend to discover," she said. "You can only tell them what you overheard, no more, no less. Got it?"

"Got it," Fran answered.

I nudged him with my elbow. "So much for your wicked woman in black."

A couple of the other employees had questions before Eileen dismissed us. "Stick around, Liz," she said. "I want to trace the route you'll take after you find the body."

While Fran waited in the lobby, Eileen and I took an elevator up to the second floor and got off. As the elevator doors closed behind us I glanced down the empty hallway. This floor was creepy too. Was the whole hotel haunted? *Don't be silly,* I told myself. *Any empty hotel hallway, with its double row of closed doors, is scary. Who's behind the doors? Is someone suddenly going to burst out and—*

I was beginning to get goose bumps, so I was glad when Eileen broke into my thoughts. "This is the plan," she said. "You'll come up here just before eight-thirty. One of the people in security will make sure you have an elevator to yourself. Everyone who's participating in the mystery should be at the party, but just in case someone's wandering around we'll try to take care of that possibility. Press the *stop* and the *door open* buttons, which will keep the elevator out of service. At exactly eight-thirty take the elevator back down to the lobby."

"There's a problem," I said. "Anyone who's waiting for an elevator will be able to see from the directional lights over the elevator that I was only on the second floor. They'd also see when I went up and when I came down. There wouldn't be enough time to go to the nineteenth floor, find the body, and come back."

"I know," Eileen said, "but you wanted to stay clear of the scene of the crime. I was trying to make it easy for you."

"I'll go up to the nineteenth floor," I told her. What else could I say? "You and your mother have planned this so carefully. I don't want to spoil it." Also, I didn't want to carry a big guilt trip with me in case anything went wrong.

Eileen smiled. "Thanks, Liz. You're terrific," she said. "Okay, here's how we'll change our plans. Take the elevator to the nineteenth floor and wait about five minutes. At eight-thirty take the elevator down."

I nodded, and she punched the elevator button. "Start screaming at the top of your lungs as the elevator door opens on the lobby level. Run across the near end of the lobby and into the open doors of ballroom A, screaming all the way, and in between screams shout, 'There's a body upstairs! A dead body!' Can you do that?"

"I guess so," I answered. "Do you want me to practice screaming?"

She put a hand on my arm. "I don't think that will be

necessary," she said. "Let me tell you why you went to room nineteen twenty-seven. You'll need to know, because people will ask."

I nodded, listening carefully, and she explained, "Edgar Albert Pitts was in the health club, soaking in the hot tub, and while he was there he was reading a play. He put it on a nearby table while he went to the dressing rooms to change, and when he left he forgot the script. You telephoned his room to tell him you'd found it, and he told you he was very busy preparing for tonight's program and asked you to bring it to him. You did, found the door ajar, and discovered his body."

The elevator arrived, and we rode it to the lobby level. Eileen walked me through the path I'd take, which was easy enough for a baby to follow—as long as it was a screaming baby—and said, "I'll see you tonight. The right time, the right place. Remember, I'm counting on you."

"I'll be there," I said. As we walked out of the ballroom I added, "Good luck."

She winced and groaned. "Never wish an actor good luck. It's an old superstition that wishing good luck almost guarantees something will go wrong."

"I'm sorry," I said. "If I can't wish you good luck, what *should* I say?"

"Say, 'Break a leg,' " she answered.

"That doesn't seem very friendly."

"It's traditional, and it's friendly."

Eileen glanced toward her watch. "I've got to set up the scene of the crime and seal it off. I'll see you at the party tonight."

Fran stepped up to join me as soon as Eileen had left. "Actors are weird," I told him, "even the nice ones."

"Everybody around here is a little weird this weekend," he said. "A woman just grabbed my jacket and hissed in my ear, 'What do you know? Tell me everything you know!' and the murder hasn't even taken place yet."

My stomach rumbled, and I said to Fran, "Let's go down to the employees' cafeteria and get some dinner. At least the people there will be normal."

But we had no sooner got in line than Earl, the accountant from the business office, who was now dressed in a doorman's uniform, sidled up to us. He muttered through one side of his mouth, "Crystal Crane asked me to call a cab for her at nine-thirty this morning. She acted very . . . very"—he stopped and pulled a tightly folded sheet of paper from his pocket, opened it, read it, and finished—"very suspicious."

"Method acting," I mumbled as the "doorman" wandered off with his tray to find a table.

"I think this is going to be fun," Fran said. "That is, if nothing goes wrong."

"Just don't wish any of the actors good luck," I told him, remembering what I'd said to Eileen. "They don't like it."

"Can I wish it to you?" he asked.

"No!" I spoke too loudly, and a couple of people turned to stare at me, but all of a sudden I thought about the screaming I'd have to do, and how it would need to be timed just right and acted just right, and a cold, hard knot formed in the pit of my stomach. Mary

Elizabeth Rafferty, the klutz. What if I ruined everything?

I managed to eat a little soup, then went up to my room and brushed my hair and put on some pink lipstick to match my pink health-club T-shirt. Pink was not a great color for redheads, but it was for a health club, so I had no choice. I thought about Eileen dressed in that dramatic green flowing dress that set off her red hair. Why couldn't I look like that?

I glanced at my watch a million times. Fran had said he'd stay with me, but I didn't want him to. I had to try to relax and get into the part I was supposed to play. As eight-fifteen approached, I was both thankful that the waiting was over and scared to death because the big moment was at hand. As I walked to the elevator, my legs shook the way they had that time I'd tried riding the health club's exercise bicycle a solid half hour, nonstop.

Tina was at the elevators in the lobby to make sure that no one else got on with me, but by the time the elevator arrived at the nineteenth floor, it wasn't just my legs that were trembling. It was all of me.

I reminded myself that there were some businessmen staying on this floor, as well as the sequestered witness. I wasn't alone, so what was I afraid of?

I pressed the *stop* and the *door open* buttons, and gingerly poked my head out. The hall was just as empty as it had been before, but it wasn't as silent. As though I'd been hypnotized, my gaze was pulled to the door of the haunted room, nineteen twenty-seven. I wondered how the ghost liked having his private place used for a make-believe murder.

While I stared at the door, the knob suddenly turned, and the door slowly opened. Someone—or something—was coming out!

No one could have jabbed that *close door* button any faster than I did, and I kept my finger on it, not knowing what would happen next. Since the elevator was on stop, it didn't move, and neither did I as I listened to footsteps approach and halt right outside my elevator door. Someone must have punched the elevator button, because I heard the elevator next to mine begin to ascend.

A deep voice muttered something, so I was pretty sure it wasn't a ghost that had been in the room. Ghosts don't take elevators or grumble at elevators that aren't fast enough. Ghost or not, I had no desire to come face-to-face with whoever had been in that room.

I heard the next elevator arrive, the doors open, and the person in the hallway enter it. As it slid downward I looked at my watch. Yikes! This was supposed to be split-second timing, and it was now two minutes *after* eight-thirty. I released the elevator from *stop,* pressed the lobby button, and my elevator began to descend.

Eleventh floor . . . eighth . . . fifth . . . I opened my mouth and got ready. Third . . . second . . . My stage fright and nervousness got mixed up with all the scary feelings I had on the nineteenth floor, and I let out a whopper of a scream as the elevator door opened. I threw myself out, yelling, "There's a body on the nineteenth floor!"

My next scream was interrupted as I smashed into a man who had stopped and whirled to stare at me. I didn't just run into him, I ran over him. I was moving like an eighteen-wheeler, and the two of us went down together.

"Sorry!" I mumbled and helped pick him up. Remembering my job, I screamed again. This time he went down by himself.

In the doorway to ballroom A, Mrs. Bandini was watching me with a big, excited grin. "Yoo-hoo, Liz!" she called.

I had to ignore her. I was an actress, playing a part. Stumbling and staggering into the ballroom, where everyone had turned to see what was happening, I screamed again and yelled, "There's a body upstairs! I found a body!"

From then on I could relax. Lamar took over and announced that he'd not only investigate but would make sure the hotel was sealed off, so no one could leave until after the police arrived.

Mrs. Duffy took the microphone and began telling everyone to remain calm. They all began giggling and pulling out little notebooks, and they didn't need me any longer, so I went back out in the hall to catch my breath.

I almost collided with the man I'd knocked down a few minutes ago. He jumped out of my way and stared at me suspiciously.

"I'm sorry," I said. "I should have looked where I was going."

He glanced from me to the people inside the ballroom and back to me. "Who was that man who left here in such a hurry?" he asked.

"Lamar Boudry. He's the hotel's chief of security."

"He said the hotel was going to be sealed off."

I nodded.

"What's with those people in there? I mean, what are they doing?"

I glanced back into the room. Crystal Crane was weeping into the microphone, while Annabelle Maloney was accusing her of wanting to get rid of Mr. Pitts. "All those people with notebooks are going to help solve the crime," I said.

He looked as though he'd eaten something sickening. "They are? All of them?"

"Sure. They're the sleuths in this murder-mystery weekend."

He thought about it a moment. "A murder-mystery weekend," he said. "Oh. Yeah!" His face brightened, and without another word he walked across the lobby.

I quickly forgot him, because Eileen, dressed in a trench coat and fedora, strode past me and into the ballroom. I followed to see what would happen, and saw her mount the stairs and take the microphone. "I'm

Detective Pat Sharp, with the Houston police department," she said, with such authority I almost could have believed her. She went on to tell everyone that the crime lab and medical examiner would soon arrive, and until they had completed their investigations and given her their reports, the scene of the crime would be sealed off.

"The police department has a heavy caseload," she said, "so I'm asking all of you to help me solve this crime. I'll report to you periodically with information we've uncovered, and I hope you'll help me question the suspects and some of the hotel employees who may have witnessed something suspicious. Tomorrow morning you'll be able to visit the scene of the crime and look for clues." She then began interrogating some of the suspects, who turned into real blabbermouths, revealing all sorts of damaging information about each other and themselves, while the sleuths in the audience took notes like crazy.

I grinned at all the corny fun, wondering what a real detective—Detective Mark Jarvis, for instance—would think of Pat Sharp.

Fran stepped up beside me and put an arm around my shoulders. "You were great," he said. "Have you considered a career as an actress?"

"Screaming in horror movies?"

"There are enough to make it a steady living."

"I'll keep it in mind," I told him.

A cart rolled up into the hallway behind us, and a couple of hotel employees began setting up easels with large sheets of paper clipped to them. Detective Sharp was instructing everyone to sign up outside—ten to a team—and they were all headed our way, so Fran and I got out of there in a hurry.

Mrs. Duffy joined us, complimented me on my scream, and said, "Why don't the two of you come upstairs with me? We'll have some soft drinks and munch on some peanuts, and Mary Elizabeth can tell me about the real body she found at the beginning of the summer."

Fran and I didn't have anything else to do, and I was kind of excited, hoping my story really would end up in a book, the way Tina had said, so we accepted. But in the elevator I remembered about someone being on the crime scene.

"There's something I need to tell you about that room nineteen twenty-seven," I said.

Mrs. Duffy didn't let me finish. "You mustn't let your imagination lure you into believing in ghosts," she said. "Just keep telling yourself, there are no such things as ghosts. There are no such things as ghosts."

"But—"

"I'm sure your friend, Tina, was playing a prank on you."

"But—"

"Think about all the places ghosts are supposed to haunt. With an English castle or a southern mansion I'm sure a story about a ghost adds a touch of romance, but I can't believe for a moment that any self-respecting ghost would be content to remain inside a well, or wander around in a barn, or haunt a toilet."

I had been trying to tell her about someone having

been in the crime scene room, but what she'd said distracted me completely. "A haunted toilet?" I asked.

"Oh yes, somewhere in a German castle."

"Where did you hear that?" Fran asked.

"I read it in one of those newspapers they sell at grocery checkout counters," she said. "Now, to get back to Mary Elizabeth's concerns . . ."

The elevator door opened on the nineteenth floor, and as we all marched out, Mrs. Duffy said, "Oh. There's Randolph Hamilton. If he's looking for me, he's at the wrong door."

Randolph, decked out in his fake wig and mustache, stood outside room nineteen twenty-nine, the other side of the scene of the crime, and as we watched he knocked at the door.

The door opened, and we heard the most gosh-awful scream coming from just inside. I had thought mine was good, but this one was even more terrified.

Randolph staggered back, as though he'd been socked. "Where's Mrs. Duffy?" he cried.

From inside the room we could hear a woman loudly going bonkers, yelling, "Help! He's after me!"

The policewoman we'd seen earlier said something to calm the other woman, then poked her head out the door and stared hard at Randolph. "I'd like some identification," she demanded.

Mrs. Duffy hurried forward. "Randolph!" she said, "you had the wrong room."

"You told us to take a good look at the scene of the crime, so we'd know where everything was," Randolph told Mrs. Duffy. "I was only trying to find you so I could get in."

"You could have got in without me," Mrs. Duffy said. "I put tape across the door lock, so all the actors could get in without a key."

"What's all this about a scene of the crime?" the policewoman demanded. "And where's the I.D. I asked for?"

Mrs. Duffy put an arm around Randolph's shoulders, as though she were protecting him, and said to the policewoman, "This is Randolph Hamilton, one of our actors in the murder-mystery weekend going on at the hotel."

It took a while to convince the policewoman that everything was all right, especially since the name on Randolph's driver's license was his real name and not Randolph Hamilton, but she finally gave in and went back to taking care of the witness she was protecting. That witness was weird. She'd seen Randolph earlier today, when she passed all of Eileen Duffy's actors, and she hadn't reacted. What was the matter with her now?

The four of us, our nerves shot to pieces, went to Mrs. Duffy's room to recuperate.

Once we were all seated, in a room just as elegant as the living room in nineteen twenty-seven, I took a long swallow of my cola and asked Randolph, "Why aren't you with the others, in the ballroom being interrogated?"

"I'm not supposed to be," he said. "Crystal and I had an argument, she insulted me, and I stormed off. That's in the script." He took off his shoes and wiggled his toes so energetically, it looked as if something horrible had crawled into his black socks.

For a while we rested and Mrs. Duffy talked more about ghosts and why there weren't any such things. I could tell that she wanted to be sure she'd convinced me before she gave up, but I wished she'd get interested in something else.

Randolph finished his soft drink, glanced at his watch, and put his shoes on again. "I'm going down to my room and go over my script. I had two commercials to make last week, and missed some of Eileen's rehearsals. I want to make sure I've got my lines down for tomorrow's scenes."

He was a nice guy, so I told him to break both his legs. He looked at me a little oddly, but thanked me anyway.

As soon as Randolph had left, Mrs. Duffy brought out a huge handbag and began rummaging through it. "Wait until I find my notebook," she said, "then Mary Elizabeth can tell me more about that murder in the Ridley at the beginning of the summer."

"More?" I asked.

"That nice Lamar, your hotel's chief of security, told me a little about it, but I want to hear your version," she said.

She suddenly looked up. "Oh, dear. I remember now. I left the notebook next door, in the crime scene. I set up the dressmaker's dummy in the dining room, and I put the notebook on the table."

"Why did you put the dummy in the dining room?" I asked.

Mrs. Duffy smiled and winked. "It's a clue," she said.

Her smile became even broader as she added, "Mary Elizabeth, be a dear and get my notebook for me, will you? I think I left it on the dining-room table." Shc held out one of the hotel's room keys and smiled. "And if the tape is still on the door lock, will you please remove it? Here's the key in case you accidentally lock yourself out."

I didn't smile back. Mrs. Duffy may not have believed there was a ghost in that room, but I did.

Fran—wonderful Fran—stood up and reached for the key. "I'll get your notebook," he said.

"Let Mary Elizabeth do it," she said. "By now, she's lost her fear of ghosts because she knows they're simply imaginary. This will give her a chance to prove to herself that she's Mary Elizabeth the Brave."

"Frankly," I said, "I'm Liz the Lily-livered. It was hard enough to go into that haunted room in the daylight. I really don't want to go by myself at night."

Mrs. Duffy looked disappointed. "Very well, I'll take care of things myself."

"You don't need to," I said as I stood up. "Fran and I can go together. Okay?"

"Thank you," Mrs. Duffy said, and began to look hopeful. "I suppose that might be a step in the right direction."

I took the key to nineteen twenty-seven, clutching it tightly, and we walked—a little more slowly than usual—the short distance to the door.

The tape was gone, so as I unlocked the door I said, "I didn't get a chance to tell Mrs. Duffy that when I'd come up here on the elevator I saw someone leaving this room."

"Who?"

"I don't know. I was so scared, I closed my elevator door."

"It was probably one of the actors," he said.

"It couldn't have been. They were all downstairs."

By this time I'd opened the door wide, and we'd stepped inside. Fran was on the side with the light switch, and I said, "The master switch is there. You can turn on all the lights in the suite."

"There are a lot of switches here," Fran said and kept flicking them on and off, trying to find the right one.

I stepped past him into the living room, ready to run for the notebook and get out of there in a hurry, the minute he found the master switch and turned on all the lights. But the bedroom light flashed and went out, the dining-room chandelier burst into light, then disappeared, and all the while Fran mumbled to himself.

However, I had seen, in those brief moments of light, something puzzling on the floor in the living room. "I thought Eileen Duffy told us they had only a tape marking the body," I said to Fran.

"That's right," Fran said. He managed to find the right switch, and the entire suite became bright with light.

I could feel a sour taste come up in my throat, and my stomach began to hurt. "Then what's that body doing on the floor?" I whispered.

Fran gave a loud gulp and moved forward. Since I was between him and the body, I moved forward too. A man was lying crumpled on his face, his head turned to one side, but as we got close enough we could see the thick, dark hair and tidy mustache . . . and the blood matted at the back of his head.

I clutched Fran around the neck, so dizzy with fear I thought I might faint. "It can't be!" I screeched. "Oh, no! It can't be!"

"It is," Fran answered, his voice cracking. "It's that actor we were just talking to—Randolph Hamilton!"

Fran and I left that room in a hurry. He ran to tell Mrs. Duffy what had happened, while I stabbed at the elevator button. Luckily, an elevator arrived in just a few seconds, so I flung myself in and rode it to the lobby floor.

The lobby was filled with the people who were playing the mystery game. In the midst of them I could see the stiff, broad-shouldered figure of Lamar Boudry, who was in conversation with Detective Pat Sharp, and the breath I'd been holding came out in a loud hiccough of relief.

But he turned and began walking away.

Frantically, I shouted, "Mr. Boudry! Wait, Mr. Boudry! You've got to come upstairs! There's been a murder!"

Mrs. Bandini and Mrs. Larabee detached themselves from the crowd and elbowed their way toward me. "Another murder!" Mrs. Bandini yelled excitedly.

Everyone in the lobby had heard, and now they all raced toward me.

"Help!" I yelled, and flattened myself against the wall. My mom was going to be really mad if I got trampled to death.

"Where was it?" someone screeched.

"Who was it?"

"What happened?"

Everyone was shouting questions at me at the same time, and I was trapped.

"Don't tell everybody, Liz. Just tell our team," Mrs. Bandini said as she and Mrs. Larabee tried to make a human wall to shield me. "Goodness knows we are handicapped by having a member on our team who thinks that Agatha Crispy is some kind of cookie."

"How can I know who you mean if you don't pronounce her name right?" Mrs. Larabee complained.

"Move back, please." The voice was so authoritative that the crowd parted without question. I was never so glad to see Lamar Boudry in my life.

"What's the problem, Liz?" he asked in a tone that implied I'd better come up with a good one . . . or else.

The crowd immediately quieted, many of them leaning toward me, all of them listening intently—all of them, that is, except the man I'd smashed into earlier. His face was bleached white, his lower lip trembled, and he tried to edge his way out of the crowd. I hoped he'd make it. He looked like he was going to be awfully sick.

"Can I tell you in private?" I asked Lamar.

"No fair!" a few of the people around us shouted.

Eileen had reached us by this time, and she didn't look very happy. "This isn't in the script," she mouthed at me.

"I know," I said, miserable that her mystery weekend was being ruined, and doubly miserable that I was the one who had to ruin it. "I can't help it, but there's a dead body upstairs in room nineteen twenty-seven."

The man in the Sherlock Holmes hat twisted his mouth in disgust. "You already told us that," he said.

I shook my head. "This is for real."

"Wait," Mrs. Bandini said. "Think carefully, Liz. Are you saying there are *two* bodies in room nineteen twenty-seven?"

"Uh—that depends," I answered.

"Mr. Pitts is one of them," she said. "Who's the other?"

I gulped and closed my eyes, remembering that I'd been speaking to him just a short time ago. "Randolph Hamilton," I answered.

Everyone began talking and writing notes like crazy, but Eileen put her lips up against my ear and said, "This is decidedly not in the script! What do you think you're doing?"

I clutched her hand. "Please believe me," I begged. "You and Lamar had better come upstairs in a hurry! This isn't make-believe. Just like I told you—Randolph Hamilton is dead."

Eileen's eyes widened, and she gave a little gasp, but immediately she became Pat Sharp the detective. "We'd better look into this, Mr. Boudry," she said. She took my hand and dragged me into the nearest elevator.

The entire group of mystery sleuths tried to crowd in with us, but Lamar gave them one of his Clint Eastwood-type, don't-you-dare-try looks and said, "No one—I repeat no one—is allowed on the nineteenth floor until you are given permission, and that won't be until tomorrow morning."

Everybody backed off in a hurry, and the three of us rode the elevator to the nineteenth floor.

Mrs. Duffy and Fran were waiting for us outside room nineteen twenty-seven in the hall.

"Mom?" Eileen asked her mother. "What happened?" She didn't look like a detective now. There were tears in her eyes, and her hands were trembling.

"I don't know any more than you do," Mrs. Duffy said. "The door automatically locked when Mary Elizabeth and Fran left, and we didn't have a key to get in."

"What did I do with the key?" I asked aloud, but Lamar simply stepped forward, pulled out his passkey, and opened the door.

The room was just as we had left it. The lights blazed brightly, and the body of Randolph Hamilton lay in the middle of the living-room floor.

Eileen let out a cry and ran to the body, dropping to her knees.

"Don't touch anything," Lamar said. He felt for a pulse at Randolph's neck, then stood up, shaking his head. He picked up the phone on the desk and called the police.

Both Mrs. Duffy and Eileen began to cry, and I felt so sick to my stomach I just wanted to get out of there, but I couldn't.

"There's something I'd better tell you about this room," I began.

But Lamar scowled and said, "Not now. Wait until the police come. You can tell them."

"It's not right that he should lie here in that silly wig and mustache," Eileen sobbed, and reached out toward Randolph's face.

"I said, don't touch—" Lamar began, but Eileen had already jerked her hand away. She fell back on the carpet with a thump.

"It's not a wig!" she cried in amazement. "It's not a fake mustache!"

We all crowded around the body and stared. "It's not John," Mrs. Duffy whispered.

"You mean Randolph?" Fran asked.

"I mean John Wallgood," she said. "Randolph is the name of the character John is playing."

"Who is this man?" Eileen asked as she climbed to her feet and moved away from the body. "He looks so much like John—uh—John's Randolph."

No one answered, but in the silence I began to remember a couple of things, and they added up.

"I think I know someone who can tell us," I said. "The sequestered witness."

They all stared at me. "You're mistaken, Mary Elizabeth. I don't have a sequestered witness in my script," Mrs. Duffy said.

"Not in your script," I said. "Next door in room nineteen twenty-nine. Lamar can tell you about her."

After a puzzled look at me, Lamar did tell us about

the witness, and I listened carefully, because I didn't know much about her either.

The woman's name was Stephanie Harmon, and she worked as secretary to a man who was going on trial for taking part in stealing security bonds from England and trying to launder the money by passing it through what they call *offshore banks* in the Cayman Islands.

At least now I knew a little bit about what laundering money meant, but I asked, "What are offshore banks? What does all that mean?"

"The Cayman Islands are a tiny group of British-owned islands in the Caribbean," Lamar said. "On the main island there are a few resort hotels, some restaurants, shops for the tourists who come from the cruise ships, and there are hundreds of banks."

"Why do the people who live there need so many banks?"

"They don't. It's other people who use them. A great deal of money flows through those banks, often on to Swiss banks with their secret accounts. Much of the money is illegal or is sent to evade paying income taxes."

"The banks there can do this?"

"They do it," Lamar said and smiled. "A friend of mine in the feds nailed a guy who claimed to be broke, but who was suspected of salting money in the Caymans. The only contact made is by phone, when account holders call the last day of the month to see what their bank balances are. My friend subpoenaed the guy's long-distance phone bills and found that, sure enough, on the last day of the month he'd called his

Cayman Island bank. Since the feds then knew the name of the bank, they were able to take it from there, and the guy was later convicted of tax evasion."

"What's Miss Harmon so scared about?" I asked. "Does she think she's going to be arrested too?"

"According to what I was told, Miss Harmon claimed to be unaware of any illegalities in what her boss was doing," Lamar said.

"How could that be? Wouldn't she have access to his files, write this letters, and all that stuff?"

"Miss Harmon's boss was a financial consultant," Lamar answered, "and much of the business with which he was involved was legitimate. It's possible he could have kept her from seeing any transactions which weren't."

"If she didn't know what he was doing was illegal, then how can she be a witness?" I asked.

"She can name names, identify some of the people who came to the office—that sort of thing."

"But if she doesn't know what kind of business these people did, then she wouldn't be able to prove it was illegal. They could have come to try to sell office supplies."

Lamar sighed patiently, which really meant he was getting impatient in a hurry. "You're nit-picking," he told me.

"I just can't understand why she's scared herself into being a gibbering basket case. She thinks someone is after her. If she doesn't know anything about what was going on, then why would anyone be after her?"

"I don't think Miss Harmon needs any more of your analyzing," Lamar said. "I'd like to hear you explain why you think she knows the identity of this murder victim."

"She saw all the actors when you were taking her into the back door of the hotel. Remember?"

He nodded, and I said, "But when Randolph knocked at her door by mistake and the policewoman answered, Miss Harmon screamed her head off."

No one reacted, so I said, "Don't you see? Randolph looked different. The second time he was wearing his wig and mustache and looked like this man."

"Liz is right!" Fran said. "I was there both times, and that's exactly what happened."

Mrs. Duffy broke in, asking Lamar, "Why don't you ask the policewoman to bring Miss Harmon over here and see if she can identify this man?"

We all took another look at the man on the floor, and I shuddered, fighting back the nausea again.

"Whether or not to bring Miss Harmon here will be the decision of the HPD detective," Lamar said.

The phone rang, and we all jumped, but Lamar took it, spoke briefly, and hung up. "That was the front desk," he said. "Detective Mark Jarvis has arrived. He's on his way up."

Detective Jarvis! Great! Detective Jarvis had been in charge of the investigation of Mr. Kamara's murder at the Ridley Hotel, and I liked him. He'd certainly be surprised to see me at the scene of the crime of this second murder.

But a few minutes later, when Detective Jarvis entered the room, along with some other police personnel, he glanced in my direction and said, "Well, I'm not surprised to see you here, Liz Rafferty. Have you solved the murder yet?"

"No," I said, "but I think I've found someone who can tell us who this man is."

Jarvis was just as I remembered him—tall, large boned, and muscular, with sun-bleached hair and a face that was more rugged than handsome, unless you thought rugged *was* handsome, which Eileen Duffy seemed to be thinking, judging from the expression on her face. Jarvis looked carefully at each person in our group. "Okay," he asked. "Which one of you is here to I.D. the body?"

"No one," Lamar answered. "It's a sequestered witness in the next room."

"These are people who have come to the Ridley for a murder-mystery weekend," I told Jarvis, and introduced Mrs. Duffy as the famous mystery writer and her daughter, Eileen, as the actress-director who was playing a detective from Houston homicide.

Detective Jarvis winced. "In a trench coat and fedora hat?" he mumbled. "What makes you think any self-respecting detective would wear a getup like that?"

"The mystery fans like it," Eileen answered, "and so do I. It sets me apart and establishes my character's job."

Jarvis shrugged. "At least you haven't got a badge."

Without batting a long eyelash, Eileen turned back the lapel of her coat to show the shiny metal detective badge that was pinned there.

"Huh," Jarvis grunted. "That badge looks like it came from Toys Aplenty."

"That's where I got it," Eileen said and her grin was so filled with mischief that Jarvis grinned back.

I thought he seemed more interested in Eileen Duffy than in the body he was supposed to be investigating, but he did get to work, conferring with the other officers, some of whom were with the crime lab. I tried not to look in their direction, pretending that there *hadn't* been a murder and there *wasn't* a dead body on the floor, but it was impossible.

Jarvis studied the wallet that was found in the victim's pocket and its contents. "Plenty of money here," he said to one of the other officers, "and he's wearing an expensive watch and ring, so it doesn't look as though the motive was robbery."

A police photographer took photos of the body from all angles, and finally Jarvis left the room and came back with Stephanie Harmon and the policewoman, whom he introduced as Maria Estavez.

With wild eyes, Miss Harmon checked out all the bodies standing up before she looked at the one on the floor. She seemed reassured at being surrounded by police officers, so she allowed Detective Jarvis to lead her over to the corpse.

For a long moment she stared, then she glanced up and nodded her head. "This man had dealings with my boss," she said.

"What's his name?"

"I don't know," she answered. "He came to the office a number of times, but whatever business was conducted wasn't recorded. I never heard his name."

"You have no idea what kind of business your former boss was doing with this man?"

"None." She whimpered and murmured, "I could be lying there instead of that poor man. How do we know the murderer wasn't after *me*?" She walked to one side of the glass door in the dining room and rested her forehead against the glass as she stared out at the roof-tops.

In a low voice Officer Estavez said to Detective Jarvis, "I hope she doesn't go to pieces before the trial is over. I suggested she try to rest, and she finally did go to her bedroom and nap just a little while ago."

"Do you have to stay with her every second?" I asked. "I mean, like, do you have to sit by her bed when she's sleeping? Or what if you have to leave to go to the bathroom?"

Estavez answered me patiently, although she didn't look very patient. "I'm not right at her side every minute. I just stay in the suite with her. I make sure the doors are locked and don't allow anyone inside unless I know who they are."

"Do you have to do that until the trial is over?"

"There are three of us assigned to Stephanie," she said. "We'll each work an eight-hour shift, although I'm doing a little overtime on this first one. Another policewoman will take my place tomorrow morning."

One of the policemen came out of the bedroom and walked to the glass door where Stephanie was standing. She apologized and moved aside as he checked the lock, and he said to Jarvis, "Both of the sliding glass doors onto the balcony are locked. Looks like entry had to come from the door to the hallway."

Jarvis began to talk to him about something else, and Officer Estavez turned to survey the living room and dining room of the suite. "This is a lot like our suite," she said, "except for a couple of strange items. What's that dressmaker's dummy in a tuxedo doing in the dining room?"

"It's a clue," Mrs. Duffy told her.

"A clue to what?"

"I can't tell you. It's something the people who are trying to solve the murder of Edgar Albert Pitts have to figure out."

"How'd you learn this guy is named Edgar Albert Pitts?"

"He's not. Pitts is just a character."

Officer Estavez's eyes narrowed, and she turned to Detective Jarvis. "Nobody told me about Pitts. When did that happen?"

Mrs. Duffy answered for him. "It didn't really. Remember, I told you about our mystery weekend? It's all make-believe for people who want to try to solve a crime."

Estavez rolled her eyes. "We haven't got enough crime on the streets? You have to make one up?" Her glance moved to Eileen, and she added, "Who are you supposed to be?"

This time Jarvis beat Eileen to an answer. "She's a homicide detective."

"Yeah, well, sure," Estavez said. "And I'm a Ninja Turtle."

Stephanie Harmon came to Jarvis and clutched his arm. Her fingers were bleached white, and I could see them tremble. "Could I please go back to my room now?" she asked.

"Of course," Detective Jarvis told her.

Harmon and Estavez left, and Jarvis talked for a minute with the other officers. When he came back to where the rest of us were waiting he said, "It looks like the weapon was the bronze paperweight on the desk. The lab will run tests on the blood smears and check for fingerprints."

Something puzzled me, so I said to Jarvis, "You asked Miss Harmon if she knew that man's name. Wasn't his name in his wallet? Didn't he have a driver's license or credit cards with his name on them?"

"Of course he did," Jarvis answered, "but I wasn't informing Miss Harmon. I was asking her. And now I'm going to ask you something. The victim's name was Frank Devane. Does that mean anything to any of you?"

Frank? Fran and I looked at each other. "Did he have a friend named Al?" I asked.

"Would you like to explain that?" Jarvis asked.

"All right," I said. This was murder, so whether I liked it or not—and I didn't—I had to be honest about what Fran and I had been doing. "You see, earlier this afternoon Fran and I were under a table and we overheard—"

"You were *under* a table?"

"We dropped into an empty conference room to snack from the leftovers and heard someone coming and hid under the serving table." The disapproval in

Lamar Boudry's face was punishment enough. "Anyhow," I said, determined to go on, "two men came into the room. They called each other Frank and Al."

"Can you describe either of them?"

"Frank had a deep voice. Al had a kind of so-so voice. Nothing special. One of them had sticky shoes."

"Can you clarify that?"

"Just the toes."

"I mean, what made you think his shoes were sticky? Did they stick to the carpet?"

"No, no. I told you, just the toes were sticky, where I poured cola on them."

Fran spoke up. "Ask the busboys, and you'll find out which one was there. One of them came into the room to clean up and the men told him they were just leaving. The busboy saw the spilled cola and left to get some wet towels to clean it up, and we got out of there before he came back."

Detective Jarvis asked, "Did you overhear any of their conversation?"

"A little," I said. "They were talking about doing something which didn't sound very honest. They didn't say what it was."

"Did they mention any names?"

"Yes," I answered. "A Mr. Yamoto and a Mr. Logan." I gave a worried look to Lamar, which wasn't any help. "And Mr. Parmegan, who's the manager of the Ridley Hotel."

"Do you think Mr. Parmegan would know this man?"

Fran and I both nodded, so Jarvis asked Lamar if he

could find Mr. Parmegan and bring him up here before they took the body away.

A medical examiner from the coroner's office arrived, along with some other official-looking people, two of whom were wheeling a stretcher. The suite, large as it was, was getting crowded, so—to my relief—Mrs. Duffy asked if we could all be excused.

Detective Jarvis granted his permission. "I think we may have covered all we need for now," he said.

"Not all we need," I told him, and I related what had happened when I took the elevator up to the nineteenth floor at eight-thirty. There was something else that was beginning to tickle the back of my mind, but I couldn't grasp it.

"It could have been the murderer leaving the scene," Jarvis said. "Did you see anything that could give us a clue to his identity?"

I started to say that I hadn't, but then I remembered how he mumbled to himself because he was impatient for the elevator to arrive. "It was a deep voice, so we definitely know the murderer wasn't a woman," I said, feeling proud of myself for reaching that conclusion.

"A deep voice," he said. "As deep as Cher's?"

"Okay," I said, my bubble popping. "It could have been Cher."

Eileen stepped forward and asked Jarvis, "Do you want us to cancel the mystery weekend?"

"The people who have signed up for it stay here all weekend, don't they?"

"Yes."

"Will they be upset by the real murder?"

"They probably won't know about it. They're kept so busy they don't have time to read newspapers or watch TV."

"Then, if Mr. Parmegan has no objections, why don't you keep it going? I'd prefer having your actors and the people playing the game close at hand. Some of them may have seen or heard something that might help with this case."

Someone like me, I thought. *What was it that was nagging at me, wanting me to remember?*

"Mr. Parmegan won't have any objections," Fran offered. "He'd hate having to give refunds to one hundred and fifty guests who paid in advance."

Eileen turned to her mother. "What are we going to do about Liz telling everyone that there were *two* bodies and that Randolph was murdered?"

"Oh, that is a problem," Mrs. Duffy said. She thought a moment and looked up, smiling. "I have it. Randolph went to the scene of the crime to see if he'd left any incriminating evidence, and someone hit him on the head, knocking him unconscious. That's when Mary Elizabeth came along, and saw him, and assumed he'd been murdered. Fortunately, Randolph has already recovered."

I was amazed that she could come up with an answer just like that. Of course, Mrs. Duffy was a mystery writer, and mystery writers have to be especially clever.

"Who hit Randolph?" Eileen asked. "Our other suspects were all in plain sight in the lobby."

Mrs. Duffy frowned as she thought, and I expected her to come up with another perfect solution, but finally she said, "Oh, never mind for now. I'll work that out later."

"I'll get back to the party," Eileen said to her mother, "and I'd appreciate it if you'd telephone John—uh—Randolph and tell him what happened and how we're going to cover it."

"Fine," Mrs. Duffy said.

"I'll walk to the elevator with you," Detective Jarvis said to Eileen. "There are a few things I'd like to ask you."

Like her telephone number, I thought.

After they'd left I said to Mrs. Duffy, "You told us that Randolph had left some incriminating evidence. Does that mean he's the one who murdered Edgar Albert Pitts?"

"Oh, no," she answered. "Every one of the suspects was at the scene of the crime and left something incriminating. One of them left a business card; one a threatening note, which is crumpled up under the desk; one left a—"

The men from the crime lab straightened, and one of them said, "Ma'am? You put those things in this room?"

"Yes," she said. "They're our clues."

"We just collected them," he said. He held up a small plastic envelope with a couple of colored cigarette butts in it.

"Oh, dear," Mrs. Duffy said. "Well, the cigarettes don't matter, but you'll have to give back our business card and letter, because I don't have duplicates, and don't touch our dummy."

The officers looked at each other. I knew what they wanted to say. But one of them asked, "Why don't you come over here, ma'am, and we'll go through these things together?"

"Come to think of it," Mrs. Duffy said, "you'll have to give back our scene of the crime. One hundred and fifty people are going to go through this room tomorrow."

"Over somebody's dead body," the officer muttered.

"Of course. That's the point, isn't it?"

Something clicked in my mind, and I said to Fran, "Come on, let's get out of here. I've got something to think about."

"Moonlight over the swimming pool?" he asked and took my hand.

I hesitated at the doorway. It was a tempting idea. "Not yet," I told him reluctantly. "I have to talk to Mrs. Bandini first."

"Why Mrs. Bandini?"

"Because," I said, "the more I think about it, the more I wonder if the two of us might have seen the murderer."

The moment we arrived in the lobby I headed for the registration desk, passing some people with television cameras and notebooks who were on their way to the elevators.

"Isn't this all too, too authentic!" I heard someone squeal.

Since Fran had spotted Mrs. Bandini and was moving in the opposite direction, I almost pulled him off his feet.

"I thought you wanted to talk to Mrs. Bandini," he complained as he staggered into me.

"I do, but I need to find out something first," I said.

At this hour the desk wasn't busy, so I motioned to Phyllis and asked, "Wasn't there a special registration line for the people coming to the murder-mystery weekend?"

"Yes," she said. "Ask me if any of the suspects were particularly demanding when they registered. I've got my answer down pat."

"No, thanks," I told her. "I'd rather ask if there were any add-ons to the list."

Phyllis shrugged. "I can check it. The list is right over here somewhere." She quickly found it and came back with it in her hand. "No add-ons," she said. "All one hundred and fifty in place. Make that one forty-nine. A man's wife couldn't come at the last minute."

That ruined the theory I was working on. "Thanks," I said and began to turn away. But I had another thought. "Who was handling this special registration?"

"Andy," she said. "He's still here. Do you want to talk to him?"

"Oh, yes!" I answered.

Phyllis brought Andy over, and I asked him, "Did any of the mystery-weekend sleuths register late, like after the party began?"

Andy nodded. He took the list and went over the names. "Mr. And Mrs. Gruin," he said. "They flew in from Dallas, and their flight was late. They came just as everybody was going into the ballroom." He ran a finger down the list and looked up. "Mr. Walters arrived even later. He was the last on the list."

"He told you his name and said he was on the list?"

"Sure." Andy looked puzzled. "Well, it wasn't exactly like that. He came up to the desk and said he was here for the mystery weekend. Since there was only one name not checked off, I said, 'Then you must be Mr. Jay Walters, but you canceled for you and your wife this morning.' And he said, 'Somebody made a mistake. I canceled for my wife but not for myself.' So I made a name tag for him and told him where he could join the mystery-weekend party."

I was beginning to get excited. "Do you remember, Andy, was this before or after I screamed?"

"After," he said. "What a racket!"

Now I was sure. I was practically jumping up and down. "Tell me, Andy. What does Mr. Walters look like?"

Andy frowned as he thought, then he shrugged. "I dunno. He's sort of average height. Kind of light hair. Had on a white sport shirt, I think."

"Thanks," I told Andy. "I know the guy you mean."

Fran and I had no sooner turned away from the desk than Mrs. Bandini jogged up to us, her friend, Mrs. Larabee, trailing in her wake.

"Liz!" Mrs. Bandini cried. "We heard about how you jumped to conclusions and thought Randolph Hamilton had been murdered. Don't let it bother you. Anyone could have made the same mistake."

"Unless they were sensible enough to feel for a pulse," Mrs. Larabee added. "Did that thought occur to you?"

"I'm sorry," I said. "I guess I panicked."

"Next time, remember," she told me.

Fran shook his head sorrowfully. "Don't count on it," he said. "Liz sometimes gets flaky in moments of stress."

Mrs. Bandini patted my arm. "Never mind. She's a dear, sweet girl who would make a wonderful granddaughter, I should be so lucky. Opal and I think we've solved the crime anyway."

"How could you solve it already?" I asked. "The game just started. Tomorrow the detective will give all of you the coroner's report and the medical examiner's report, and you'll find out more about the suspects and what motives they might have. You haven't even visited the scene of the crime."

Mrs. Bandini shrugged. "We have our own way of detecting. The pretty girl didn't murder him. Pretty girls are never the murderers. They always fall in love with somebody, or somebody falls in love with them. And the shy girl didn't commit the murder. Shy people don't commit murders. They quietly write 'I wish he was dead' in their diaries, and that's as far as they go."

"Randolph isn't the murderer," Mrs. Larabee chimed in, "because someone hit him on the head. Why would someone hit him on the head if he's the murderer? It makes no sense. Only the murderer would go around hitting people on the head."

Mrs. Bandini took control of the conversation. "They want us to think Arthur Butler murdered Mr. Pitts, because it's an old cliché that the butler did it, only some of us will say, 'Ah ha! That's in there just to trick us, so we'll say he couldn't have done it, only he really did do it.' They're not going to trap us that way."

"I didn't follow all that," I told her. "If you want to go over it again—"

"It doesn't matter," she said. "The nephew is the murderer."

Mrs. Larabee nodded enthusiastically. "It has to be. He'd inherit. Who else would inherit? Nobody."

"I wouldn't vote too soon," I told them. "You've got

until midnight tomorrow to make up your minds, and Mrs. Duffy might have a few surprises for you. Mystery writers do that to keep you off balance, so solving the crime won't be too easy."

Mrs. Larabee made a little face of disgust. "This is supposed to be realistic. So if Mrs. Duffy wants to be realistic, then she'd have the murderer be the nephew. He'd inherit. Who else would inherit?"

I couldn't argue with that, and I needed some verification from Mrs. Bandini. "Do you remember when I came screaming out of the elevator?"

"Which time?"

"Uh—the first time."

"Of course. For your sake, dear, we'll forget the second time."

"Mrs. Bandini, did you get a good look at the man I ran into?"

"Yes, indeed," she said.

I remembered the hit men who'd come into the health club, and the detailed descriptions of them that Mrs. Bandini had given Detective Jarvis when he was investigating Mr. Kamara's murder. "Could you give me a description of him?" I asked.

She smiled. "The man eats well and takes his vitamins, or he would have gotten a broken bone or two out of that collision."

"But did you—?"

"I'm getting to that," she said. "He was wearing brown slacks and a cream-colored guayabera shirt, which was probably bought in Mexico, unless he got it at Walter Pye's men's store, which carries a nice quality and sometimes has them on sale. He has light-brown hair, he's about five feet ten and a half, and I'd guess that he's around forty-five or forty-six."

"Did you see what direction he'd been coming from?"

"From the elevator," she answered. "He got off the elevator to the right of yours just a minute or two before yours landed."

I glanced at Fran and must have looked as excited as I felt, because Fran cautioned, "That still doesn't prove anything."

"He's over there with Team Number Ten," Mrs. Bandini said.

"Why don't we talk with him?" Fran asked. "Just chat with him?"

"Thanks, both of you," I said, and began to turn away, but Mrs. Bandini grabbed my arm, and Mrs. Larabee grabbed Fran's.

"Not so fast," Mrs. Larabee said. "*We're* supposed to question *you.*" She looked at Fran. "You first. Tell us what you know about the murder."

"Murder?" Startled, Fran looked at me. "I didn't think we were supposed to say anything about it."

"Edgar Albert Pitts's murder," I prompted.

"Oh," Fran said. "Okay, then," and he recited, "I took a breakfast tray up to Annabelle Maloney's room. When I got there, Crystal Crane was arguing with Annabelle, and I could see that Annabelle had been crying. Crystal was already dressed for going out. I think she said something about having an appointment, but I heard her say to Annabelle, 'You'll be in trouble if they find out.' "

"Hmmm," Mrs. Bandini said to Mrs. Larabee. "There was a movie I saw once in which a quiet, mousy woman got more grief than she could take, so she turned into a veritable tiger and committed the murder."

"But Annabelle wouldn't inherit," Mrs. Larabee said.

"Nevertheless, we should rethink our position," Mrs. Bandini told her. "Let's see what information Liz has for us."

I tried to remember every word that I was supposed to have learned as I said, "Arthur Butler came to the Ridley health club for a swim, and Martin Jones was already there, working out with the weights."

"The nephew," Mrs. Larabee said smugly.

"That's right. Mr. Butler stopped to talk, and I thought it was a friendly chat, but when I was carrying an armful of towels through the room I passed them and overheard Mr. Jones laugh and say, 'Call it blackmail if you like. You can call it anything you want. Just be sure you come up with the payment on time.' Mr. Butler was really angry."

Mrs. Larabee gave a shriek of delight, and both women began writing as fast as they could in their notebooks.

Fran and I excused ourselves and made our way through the crowd, stopping now and then to give our information to other sleuths who wanted to question us. Everyone's attention was diverted for a moment by a noisy man who was obviously drunk and who was being led out of the hotel's crowded bar by Tina.

"I'm not drunk!" he was shouting. "I've only been there since seven o'clock!"

"I'll escort you to your room, sir," Tina said firmly, and steered him toward the elevators.

I'd never seen the man before, so I wondered why I felt there was something familiar about him, but I forgot him in a moment as I turned and found myself face-to-face with the man I'd knocked down. When he saw me his eyes shifted nervously to each side, and he tried to back up a step, only someone was behind him and he couldn't.

I wasn't sure what to do next or even what I should say, so I held out my right hand and said, "Hi. My name is Mary Elizabeth Rafferty, and this is Francis Liverpool the Third."

Mr. Walters's breathing was uneven, and his Adam's apple bounced up and down. He glanced down at the big, printed letters on his name tag before he looked up and said, "I'm Jay Malters."

"Malters? You mean Walters, don't you?" I blurted out.

He squinted and twisted the name tag until it was turned so he could read it right side up, and his shirt was all scrunched up. "Of course," he said with a sickly smile, and smoothed his shirt into place. "Walters. I guess I'm just thinking so hard about solving this mystery, I got confused."

No one gets confused over his own name. It was obvious to me that this man had forgotten the name that Andy had called him until he read it off his name tag. Upside down a *W* looks like an *M*. I was sure this was the man who had come from the scene of the crime room.

"Well, have fun," I told him. "If you want to ask Fran or me any questions, go right ahead."

He didn't have a chance to ask questions. Someone at the other end of the lobby shrieked, "They're taking Pitts's body out the back door!" And everyone in the lobby turned and raced toward the back of the hotel.

Fran and I were swept toward the elevators, where we managed to squeeze out of the pack of sleuths, but it wasn't until we were inside one of the elevators, headed for the nineteenth floor, that I said to Fran, "Mr. Walters may be the man who murdered Mr. Devane. We have to find Detective Jarvis."

"I don't get it," Fran said. "If Walters is the murderer, why didn't he just leave the hotel?"

"Think about it. Being part of the mystery-weekend group is a perfect cover for him. Who'd suspect any of the sleuths of committing a real murder? Especially when the victim has no connection at all with anybody at the mystery weekend?"

"You may be right," Fran said. "We definitely have to talk to Detective Jarvis."

We caught Jarvis just as he was leaving the scene of the crime. He was carrying Mrs. Duffy's dressmaker's dummy, and Mrs. Duffy was with him, her arms filled with odds and ends, which were undoubtedly her clues.

"Detective Jarvis," I began.

Jarvis ignored me, he was so relieved at seeing Fran.

"I'm glad you're here," he said. "You can be the dead body. Mrs. Duffy was insisting that *I* do it."

"I don't want to be a dead body," Fran told him.

"Could I say something?" I asked.

"All you have to do is lie on the floor," Mrs. Duffy told Fran. "I'll draw your outline on the rug with narrow masking tape. You'll be a stand-in for Edgar Albert Pitts."

"As you can see, we're juggling rooms," Jarvis said. "The new scene of the crime room is going to be located in the Duffys' room, and Mr. Parmegan is moving the Duffys to a room on the eighteenth floor."

"I am going to miss that lovely suite," Mrs. Duffy said.

"I hate to interrupt," I began, then said, "No. I want to interrupt. It's important to interrupt. Detective Jarvis, I think I know who murdered Mr. Devane."

As I explained my reasoning, Jarvis shoved the dummy into Fran's hands, grabbed my elbow, and steered me toward the elevators. "You can I.D. him for me," he said.

I guess I expected a big commotion as Detective Jarvis confronted Mr. Walters—or whoever he was—but it didn't work that way. As soon as I had pointed out Mr. Walters, Detective Jarvis slipped through the crowd, spoke to Mr. Walters quietly, and the two of them moved toward me.

It wasn't until we were back inside the elevator that Mr. Walters slumped against the back wall for support and said, "You want to talk to me about Frank Devane, don't you! Well, I didn't kill him!"

I gasped, and Jarvis said, "You know him, and you know he's been murdered."

"All right. I admit that much," Mr. Walters said. He was sweating so much, his shirt was getting damp. "When this girl ran out of the elevator yelling that she found a body, I thought she meant Devane. I couldn't believe it happened so fast." He threw me an angry look and said, "I was just going to walk quietly away from the hotel, and no one would have known the difference, but when she ran into me, making all that racket, it caught everyone's attention. Somebody would have remembered me."

"Mrs. Bandini did," I offered, but got nothing more than another sharp glance for my trouble.

Mr. Walters wasn't through. "I nearly panicked," he said, "but when I found out those people were playing a mystery game, I decided to join them. That would be my reason for being in the hotel, and no one would connect me with Devane."

"Would you like to call an attorney and have him present while I question you?" Jarvis asked.

Mr. Walters groaned and wiped an arm across his forehead. "You have to believe me. Devane was dead when I got there."

"What were you doing on the nineteenth floor?"

The elevator's door suddenly opened, and we stepped out into the hallway. Mr. Walters shrunk back, cringing as he looked at the door of room nineteen twenty-seven.

"I came up here to speak to Devane."

"Business?"

"Yes, business. The savings and loan he owned went under, you know, and so did all my savings."

I spoke without thinking. "I thought the money in accounts was insured."

What I'd said seemed to make Mr. Walters even more upset. "Devane had asked me to do him a favor. He had a bank customer—a developer who was overextended and unable to borrow any more from the bank—so, the way Devane explained it, I would borrow money from the bank, putting up my store as collateral, and lend it to the developer at a high interest rate through Devane. Then, after the first of the year, the developer would pay me back and I'd make a good-sized profit. Only, Devane's S and L went under, and the federal government took over the collateral—my store. I'm bankrupt. I've lost everything, and it's all Devane's fault!"

"So you came up here to get even?" Jarvis asked.

"No! Just to talk to him. I hoped we could work something out. I was headed for his room when I noticed the doorway to this . . . this room was standing open."

"The doors close automatically," I said.

"No. This was propped open with a wedge of cardboard." He reached into the side pocket of his slacks and pulled out a small rectangle of dark cardboard, which had been folded in thirds.

"Just out of curiosity, I looked inside the room and saw someone on the floor. I ran inside to see if I could help, but I saw that it was Devane, and he was dead, so I quickly shut the door."

"Why?" Detective Jarvis asked.

"I don't know. It was instinctive. I had to think. But I couldn't. I didn't know what else to do, so I got out of there and went downstairs."

"Do you think whoever killed Mr. Devane left the door open so the body would be found?" I asked. "The maid wouldn't come by for a bed turn-down, because the room was unoccupied and because of the—"

Jarvis interrupted. "There are some questions I want to ask you, Mr. Walters," he said. "We can talk in here."

Mr. Walters's shoulders slumped, and he looked totally defeated. "Forget this 'Mr. Walters' stuff. My name's Steven Burns."

Detective Jarvis pulled a key from his pocket, opened the door, and waited for Mr. Burns to enter.

I stepped forward, but Jarvis said, "You're excused, Liz. This is going to be a private conversation."

The door closed behind the two men, and I ambled down to Mrs. Duffy's room, feeling somewhat left out. I was the one who'd told Jarvis about Mr. Walters, wasn't I?

Fran let me in and pointed to the outline of his body on the floor. "Creepy, huh?" he said.

"I've called a bellman," Mrs. Duffy said. "Eileen's things and mine are packed, so he can move us now." She stopped and put a hand to her mouth. "Oh. I forgot to check the bathroom. I'm sure I packed all of Eileen's things. That is, I think I'm sure."

"I'll check it for you," I told her, and trotted down the hallway to the bathroom.

I threw open the door and gasped as I looked into Randolph Hamilton's mournful eyes. He was seated on the floor against the mirrored wall. His back was hunched over his knees, his arms wrapped around his legs.

"What are you doing in here?" I asked him.

"I wish I knew," he answered.

"Are you hiding from someone?" I persisted.

"That man who was murdered. . . . He looked like me—me in this wig and mustache, that is." Randolph let out a groan and said, "I know what happened. They got the wrong man."

"What do you mean by that?" I asked.

"It's pretty obvious, isn't it?" he said. "The murder victim was supposed to be me."

"Mrs. Duffy's ready to move out of this suite," I told Randolph. "It's the new scene of the crime."

He looked up at me, surprised, and I held out a hand. "Hiding isn't going to help, but talking with Detective Jarvis is," I said. "Come on. I'll take you to him."

"Do you really think he can help me?"

"If you tell him what you told me—and why—I'm sure he'll help you."

I felt like Randolph's mother as he trustingly put his hand in mine. Some mother! I gave him a tug to help him get up and banged his shoulder on the edge of the washbasin.

As we entered the living room of the suite, Mrs. Duffy said, "Oh my, we *were* leaving something behind. Randolph, I didn't know you were here. Eileen called just a minute ago and asked that Mary Elizabeth and Francis come downstairs, because the guests are eager to interrogate them. She was trying to find you, Randolph."

Randolph just nodded and rubbed his sore shoulder.

I looked around for Fran, and Mrs. Duffy said, "I sent Francis down immediately. When a director says 'jump,' you jump."

"I'll jump in a minute," I told her. "First, Randolph and I are going to see Detective Jarvis. Murderers have priority over directors."

"Good point," she said. "And a good line. If you don't mind, I'll use it. I'm working on a novel in which the murder takes place in a theater."

"Sure, use it," I said, feeling vaguely famous. "It's fine with me."

Mrs. Duffy looked as though she'd suddenly remembered something. "Tomorrow, Mary Elizabeth, when you have some free time, you *must* tell me about the murder you were involved in at the beginning of the summer."

"I will," I told her. I wondered, if she decided to write the story and it got published, if they'd put my picture on the cover of the book. I began to get excited, but then I realized I'd have to do something about my hair. And my eye makeup. And the shape of my nose. It was too discouraging to think about.

Mrs. Duffy shut the door, tested it, and walked to the elevators. With Randolph right behind me, I knocked at the door of room nineteen twenty-seven. Detective Jarvis opened the door and let us in.

The room felt strange and icy cold. With the terrible thing that had happened and with all those people crowded into the suite, I'd forgotten about the ghost. But I remembered it with a start—as though it were thinking of me—and found myself glancing toward the hall that led to the bedrooms, half expecting to see an ethereal figure in a long, white gown suddenly appear. Detective Jarvis's strong and solid presence was tremendously comforting.

As we entered the living room, Mr. Walters—I mean, Mr. Burns—took one goggle-eyed look at Randolph, leaped to his feet, let out a horrible, strangling sound, and fell back on the sofa. "Devane!" he rasped.

"I'm not Frank Devane," Randolph said in an aggrieved tone of voice. He turned to me. "You see, that's what I mean. The killer thought Devane was me."

Mr. Burns struggled to an upright position and asked, "If you're not Devane, who are you?"

"My name is John Wallgood." Randolph's eyes narrowed. "For that matter, who are *you*?"

"He's the man who murdered Frank Devane," I said.

Randolph's back slammed into the wall, and I could see the whites of his eyes spread all around his pupils.

"Don't disseminate misinformation, Liz," Detective Jarvis told me. "Mr. Burns has not been charged with murder."

There was another knock at the door, and Jarvis opened it to two uniformed policemen. He then turned to face Steven Burns, and spoke so firmly that Mr. Burns's head bobbled like one of those toy dogs with a spring in its neck that you sometimes see in the back of a pickup truck. "It's in your own best interest to have these men accompany you downtown, where your attorney will meet you and remain with you while another detective from our homicide department takes your statement."

Mr. Burns staggered to an upright position, still nodding, and left the room with the police officers.

"If you've caught your murderer, then the crime is solved," I told Jarvis.

"It's not that easy," Jarvis answered. "There are too many loose ends, too many things that don't add up."

"That means you don't think Mr. Burns committed the murder, doesn't it?"

"Between you and me, I don't think he did it, but we'll have to make sure." Jarvis looked from me to Randolph and back again. "Is there something I can help you with?"

"You can help Randolph," I told him. "He thinks the murderer killed Devane, thinking he was Randolph."

"Mr. Hamilton, let's sit down," Detective Jarvis said. "Would you like to explain this?" He sat on one of the sofas, causing the cushions to collapse in the middle.

"When I'm wearing this stupid wig and mustache, Devane and I look—uh—looked nearly identical," Randolph said. He dropped into a chair, his chin resting on his chest.

I leaned against the wall, out of Detective Jarvis's line of vision, and quietly listened.

"Not identical, but close," Jarvis said.

"Close enough, so the hit man got mixed up."

"What hit man are we talking about?"

Randolph closed his eyes and groaned. "I've been gambling, and most of the time it's win some, lose some. But for a while now I've had a run of bad luck, and I've had to borrow quite a bit of money." He opened his eyes and said, "You don't get money to gamble with from banks, you know."

"I know," Jarvis said.

"So these people I borrowed the money from sent me a warning to pay up, or else. I didn't. I couldn't! I guess they sent someone to carry out the threat, but they got Devane instead of me."

Detective Jarvis and Randolph talked about what was said, how it was said, how much money—all kinds of stuff that Jarvis had to know, I guess, but it got pretty boring after a while. He finally said, "There's a possibility that you're right, but there's a much greater possibility that Devane, himself, was the target. So far we've learned that as the former owner of a failed savings-and-loan institution he was involved in many financial ventures, some of which were not successful, some maybe not even legal, and along the way he's probably made enemies. I don't think you've got anything to worry about."

"But is there a chance I'm right?"

Jarvis nodded. "I have to admit there's a slight one."

Randolph shook his head. "I can't let Eileen down right in the middle of her mystery weekend," he said, "but I haven't got enough courage to go downstairs and face all those people. I keep thinking that the murderer will hear about who really got killed and come back for me."

Suddenly, his face brightened and he sat upright. "None of the people playing the mystery game were told about the real murder, were they?"

"No," Jarvis said. "We're not hiding it from them.

We're just not talking about it. I think it's better that the weekend continue as planned."

"All right, then," Randolph said, his voice rising in excitement. "Could you keep the murder from the press too? I mean, if the killer doesn't find out about it . . ."

He looked so hopeful that I had to help him. "That's a great idea, Detective Jarvis," I said. "Total secrecy."

Jarvis swiveled and glared at me. "You don't belong here," he said. "This is a private conversation, and Mr. Hamilton's idea is not a great idea. It's an impossibility."

Randolph pressed the palms of his hands against his forehead. "Then what am I going to do?" he moaned.

"We'll find out what we can," Jarvis said, "and in the meantime I'll ask for a plainclothes officer to be stationed among the mystery sleuths to keep an eye on you."

"Terrific!" I said.

"Out!" Detective Jarvis pointed toward the door. He didn't look too happy with me, so I left in a hurry.

Downstairs the crowd had thinned out quite a bit, but the excitement had heightened.

Mrs. Bandini, still going strong, made her way to me. "They arrested Mr. Walters," she said. "Right out of his team! Two officers led him away!"

Mrs. Larabee puffed up behind her. "None of us are safe," she said. "I didn't know there would be this much audience participation."

I leaned down to whisper. "You're safe enough. Mr. Walters was . . . was one of the actors."

"Oh!" Mrs. Bandini exclaimed, her eyes shining. "Was he the murderer?"

I only wanted to put them at ease, not lead them too far astray. "Shhh," I said. "Just between you and me, Mr. Walters didn't kill Edgar Albert Pitts. He's only a red herring."

Mrs. Larabee tugged at her friend's sleeve. "Just how do herrings fit into a murder?"

"Red herrings are just things put into a plot in order to lead mystery fans astray," I explained.

Mrs. Larabee shrugged, but she didn't look pleased. "That's not being very nice," she said. "I didn't come here to be led astray."

I saw Eileen give a nod of her fedora to Crystal Crane, who yawned delicately, said she was exhausted, and excused herself to go to bed. There was no sign of Martin Jones or Arthur Butler, so they must have already left. Annabelle walked toward the elevators with Detective Pat Sharp, who mentioned something about further questioning, and they disappeared.

Fran popped up at my side and murmured into my ear, "The pool, the moonlight—remember? There's no time like the present."

I looked at my watch. "It's already ten-thirty. We aren't supposed to be in the health club after eleven."

"But we can stay until eleven," Fran said. His smile was so endearing, I put my hand into his, and we walked down the corridor to the Ridley health club, where two people bubbled away in the hot whirlpool tub, and a lone swimmer stroked back and forth in the enclosed section of the pool.

Deely Johnson, the health-club manager, looked up from the towels she was stacking as we strolled into the office. "Come to help?" she asked with a smile.

"No," I said. "We're just going to sit outside for a while."

"Don't forget. We close at eleven o'clock," Deely said with a wink and went back to her work.

Outside, all alone with the moon and stars and sticky humidity and a couple of mosquitos, Fran pushed two lounge chairs together, and we lay back, holding hands.

"I feel like we're on a vacation," Fran said.

"Me, too, but it's a short vacation. I've got to be available to answer questions when the health club opens tomorrow morning at eight."

"Nobody told me where I'd have to hang out, so I'll stick around the health club and watch you work."

I laughed. "You just think you will. You'll be busy answering questions from the mystery sleuths."

"I've been answering," he said, "and some of their questions are weird. One wanted to know if I'd ever seen the detective taking a bribe, somebody else asked if I was fluent in German, and a tall, skinny woman wanted to know if I knew how to ski."

"What has that got to do with Edgar Albert Pitts?"

"Don't ask me," he said. "In fact—"

"Listen, Fran," I said. "I've been thinking." I rose on my left elbow to look at him more closely. "Nobody's brought up something important. What was Frank Devane doing in the scene of the crime room? And why was he killed there, instead of in his own suite?"

Fran rose on his right elbow, and our noses were

practically touching. "Let's not talk about murder," he said, and kissed me.

He was very good at changing the subject, but at that moment the pool lights went off, and Deely called from the doorway, "Come on in. I'm locking up."

As soon as we joined her she said, "Mr. Parmegan wants to talk to you, Liz. He called down and left a message for you."

"He wants to talk to me *now*?" I looked at my watch. One minute to eleven.

"Tomorrow morning at ten," she said. "I'll be at the club, too, on account of you've got to be a witness at the mystery weekend, so there's nothing to stop you from meeting with him."

I gulped. "He heard about my being under the table and pouring cola on Al's shoes. I bet that's it. I'm going to get fired."

"He didn't sound like he was going to fire you," Deely said, but she stared at me oddly. "What were you doing under a table pouring cola on somebody?"

"It's a long story."

"I don't care how long it is," she answered.

"Some other time," I said, and walked toward the door with Fran.

Suddenly a woman leaped into my path from the shadows behind a potted ficus tree. As I stumbled back, her teammates scrambled after her. "Here she is!" the woman shouted and grabbed my arm. "They said you're a witness! They said you overheard an argument! Tell us, quick! We have to catch up with the other teams!"

"I'll tell you," I said, "but out in the hallway. The manager of the health club has to lock up."

"But we want to *see* the club. We want to see where you were and where they were and if there were any weapons around."

"Weapons?"

A man in the group nodded vigorously. "Detective Sharp told us that Edgar Albert Pitts was hit on the head with a blunt object."

Just like the real murder, I thought. How much was fiction and how much was fact? Did Mrs. Duffy have ESP when she wrote the script? Surely, there couldn't have been any way she'd know what would happen.

"Come tomorrow morning, any time after eight," I told them. "I'll show you all around the club."

It was eleven-thirty before they had finished questioning me, and Fran and I could head upstairs. "I don't get it," I told him. "What difference does it make if Pitts's nephew ordered his lunch from room service, or if he'd ever traveled to Colombia?"

"The man with the FBI sunglasses was kind of mad at you because you said you didn't know."

"I had to say I didn't know. Eileen told us we couldn't make up anything." As we got into the elevator I looked at Fran suspiciously. "Have you been making things up?"

For a moment he grinned wickedly, but then he said, "No, Liz. I promise. I'm sticking to the script."

Outside my door, as I fished into the pocket of my shorts for the key, I felt *two* keys, and as I pulled them out I realized I'd forgotten to give back the key to room nineteen twenty-seven. I palmed it, opened my door with my own key, bent my knees just a little, and kissed Fran good night.

But once inside my tiny room my mind whirled with questions. Was it just coincidence that both the make-believe victim and the real victim were murdered in the same way? Did Devane and his murderer get into the scene of the crime room while the lock was taped open? Or was it later, after the tape had been removed? In that case they'd have to use a key. Who had keys to the room besides Mrs. Duffy and Eileen? Did the ghost have anything to do with the murder? Did Mrs. Duffy? Was Fran ever going to grow taller, so I wouldn't have to bend my knees when we kissed?

First things first, I told myself. Who had a key?

As I looked at the pair of keys in the palm of my hand, I got a weird feeling in the pit of my stomach. Who had a key? I had.

I suppose I slept during the night. I must have slept, because the next morning the telephone woke me up.

I answered with a mumble, not awake enough to open either my eyes or my mouth, and heard Eileen say, "Liz? It's already seven. I thought you'd be awake."

"I'm awake," I said, and for a moment tried to figure out where I was. Suddenly it came back to me and I sat up in bed, rubbing my eyes. "Is something wrong?" I asked.

"No," she said. "Something's right. Mom fixed the script to account for Randolph's hit on the head."

"Good," I said, my confidence in Mrs. Duffy's talents returning.

"Listen carefully," Eileen said, "because this concerns you."

"I know," I said, "I told everybody he was—"

"Listen," she repeated. "This is what really happened. You went back to the nineteenth floor because you were curious about the murder. You thought that maybe one of the crime lab investigators would answer some of your questions."

"Like, what was the murder weapon?"

"Right," she said. "Very good. You've got the picture."

"Did they answer my questions?"

"No. Instead they asked *you* questions. They wanted to know how you happened to find the body, if you saw anyone else on the nineteenth floor, and if you touched anything. Got it?"

"Got it. But where does Randolph Hamilton come in?"

"Randolph Hamilton had been curious too. But he was afraid to question the police, so he hung around the hallway, trying to listen in. When you got off the elevator, he quickly stepped into that nearby broom closet so that you wouldn't see him. Do you remember where the closet is?"

"Yes."

"Unfortunately for Randolph, he knew you'd been talking to the police on the scene, and he wanted to find out what you'd learned, so as you came by on your way to the elevators, he stepped out of the closet. You were edgy in the first place, so when Randolph suddenly appeared behind you, grabbing your shoulder and speaking your name, you instinctively turned around and slugged him, knocking him out. You thought you'd killed him, so you hurried downstairs."

I didn't know what to say. "Your mother, the famous mystery writer, thought this up?"

"Don't worry. It will work."

"I don't think so," I said. "I don't think I could have hit Randolph that hard."

"You were under stress. You were also a nervous wreck. The sleuths will buy that. They know that a burst of adrenaline causes people to have unusual strength."

She was probably right about the sleuths. Last night they were accepting anything and everything, and I suppose I did act kind of weird, with all that running around and screaming.

But there was another problem. "With a room full of police at the crime scene, why did I go all the way down to the lobby to get Lamar Boudry?"

"Mom already thought of that," Eileen explained. "Remember, you thought Randolph was dead and that you had killed him, but you didn't want anyone to know you had done it. If you went down to the lobby, it would buy you some time and confuse the issue. It could have been *anyone* in that hall who did it, not just you. That's also why you told everyone at first that you'd just found Randolph. Understand?"

I hesitated. "Could I have a new name?"

"What do you mean? You're playing yourself."

"That's the point. Myself is coming across as pretty stupid."

"No, no, no," Eileen reassured me. "Remember? You were terrified, and you panicked."

"I also must have confessed everything, or no one would have figured it out."

Now there was silence on her end. "I guess you did," she said.

Remembering what Mrs. Larabee had told me, I said,

"I not only didn't feel for a pulse, to make sure Randolph was dead, but I tried to trick everyone, and then I blabbed the whole thing. Put dishonest and idiotic in there along with stupid."

Eileen sighed. "Frankly, Liz," she said, "I'd just as soon pack up my actors and go home. It's awful knowing that a real murder took place here. John—uh—Randolph's scared to death, Annabelle's hung up on that story about the ghost in room nineteen twenty-seven and jumps at the slightest sound, and Mom kept me awake half the night trying to work her plot around what you said about Randolph being dead. But Detective Jarvis asked us to stay and keep the mystery weekend going, and actors aren't kidding when they say 'the show must go on.' If they've got a job to do, no matter what happens, they do it."

"I guess I'm an actor, too, even if I am using my own name," I told her.

"I hope so," she said.

I felt kind of strange thinking about the way people would be looking at me after that story about what I had done came out, but there wasn't anything else I could do. "Okay," I said. "I'll tell them everything you told me."

"Oh, thank you, Liz!" Eileen said. "I just can't thank you enough!"

I could hear someone in Eileen's room speaking to her, but she came back to me and said, "I've got to hurry, Liz. Martin and Randolph are scheduled to have a fistfight during the breakfast buffet in the ballroom, and I've got to make sure they're ready and it comes off on schedule. I'll tell the sleuths about you when we meet for the detective's report at nine."

"Okay," I said, but as I hung up the phone I wondered how I'd let myself get into this mess.

I was supposed to show up at the health club at eight, and I wanted a big breakfast, so I quickly showered and dressed in my shorts and T-shirt uniform and hurried down to the employees' cafeteria in the basement.

Fran already had a table and a head start on scrambled eggs, bacon, and everything that went with it, but he put down his fork as I joined him and said, "How come the eggs and bacon we're eating probably came from the same hen and pig as the eggs and bacon that's being served in the hotel's dining room, only theirs tastes so good, and ours doesn't?"

"They're paying for theirs," I said.

"Good reason," Fran said, and began to eat again.

I told him about Eileen's phone call as I spread strawberry jelly on my toast and thumb.

"Wow," he said and stuffed his mouth with limp hash browns. "You are a sneaky one."

"The show must go on," I mumbled.

"So must the health club," Deely said over my shoulder. "Hurry up and finish your breakfast. I'll open up."

There were a couple of media people and a TV cameraman in the lobby as I walked through on my way to the health club. I assumed they'd come about Devane's murder, but a few of the mystery sleuths preened and giggled at the cameraman, and I heard one of them say, "This is all so realistic! Isn't it fun!"

There was a meeting with Detective Pat Sharp scheduled for eight-thirty, so none of the hotel guests who were playing the mystery game came into the health club, which gave me time to scrub the tiles and fish leaves out of the outdoor side of the pool. I expected all the sleuths to rush in after the detective's talk, point their fingers at me, and ask a million questions, but around nine o'clock only Mrs. Bandini and Mrs. Larabee hurried in, both of them a little out of breath.

They cornered me in the office, and Mrs. Bandini said, "Detective Smart isn't finished with her report yet, but we asked our teammates to take notes for us. We feel it's our duty to talk to you, Mary Elizabeth."

"About my slugging Randolph Hamilton?" I asked.

"We'll get to that later," Mrs. Larabee said. "What we have to say is more important."

The two of them looked at each other, and Mrs. Bandini spoke up. "The first time we met you, I said, 'Isn't that a lovely, sweet girl?' Didn't I say that, Opal?"

"Your very words," Mrs. Larabee said.

"And the way you helped solve the murder at the hotel in June—well, you were any mother's pride and joy."

"But last night . . ." Mrs. Larabee said. "Well, frankly, we're concerned about your behavior."

"It's just a part I'm playing," I told them, but they weren't listening.

"We're afraid this change in your formerly perfect behavior comes from bad companions," Mrs. Bandini said.

I knew who she meant. She had wanted me to date

her gorgeous grandson, Eric, and wasn't too happy that I chose Fran instead.

"I don't have bad companions," I told them, but their lips tightened and their eyes grew all-knowing, and it wasn't hard to figure out that I wasn't reaching them. These women had been my friends ever since I came to work at the Ridley health club at the beginning of summer. I didn't want them to think badly of me. What was I going to do?

I sighed and leaned back against the desk. "None of it happened the way they said," I whispered.

"What do you mean?" They both moved forward.

I raised my head and murmured, "I had to lie. I had no choice. My life is in danger."

They gasped, and I realized I might have gone just a little too far and I'd better tone it down. Eileen had told us we'd have to stick to the script. "I was told what to say, but no one must know this," I whispered. "Don't tell anyone, not even your teammates."

Their eyes shone with excitement, and Mrs. Larabee even raised her right hand as though making a pledge.

"I knew it!" Mrs. Bandini said. "I knew you wouldn't hit someone on the head, Mary Elizabeth."

"And not take his pulse." Mrs. Larabee looked smug.

"And sneak around pretending someone else killed him." Mrs. Bandini smiled and gave me a little hug. "Your secret is safe with us, Mary Elizabeth."

Mrs. Larabee tugged at the shoulder of her friend's shirt. "Let's go find the rest of our team! Quickly!"

They scurried off, leaving me with confused feelings. They didn't ask who put me in danger. They were just happier that my life was in danger than that I was dishonest. Well, at least they didn't consider Fran to be a bad companion any longer.

The telephone rang, and it was Tina. "Hi," she said. "I've got the health club on monitor. Where is everybody?"

"At the detective's meeting," I answered.

"Meeting . . . that reminds me," she said. "Lamar wanted me to remind you to be in Mr. Parmegan's office at ten o'clock on the nose."

I felt like someone had socked me in the stomach. "Lamar's going to be there too?" I asked. "What kind of big trouble am I in?"

"Nobody tells me anything," Tina said. "It's the classic power-structure syndrome. As long as you know something that someone under you doesn't know, then you have power over them."

"I've got zilch power," I said, "because I'm just a summer employee."

"That's right," Tina said cheerfully. "You're on the bottom rung."

That didn't make me feel any better. I wished Tina would hurry up and start working for that degree in psychology. She might not know any more then than she did now about what she was talking about, but at least she'd have the authority to say it.

"I'll talk to you later," I told her, hung up, and hurried to Mr. Lewis Parmegan's office.

My knees were shaking as Marie, his secretary, smilingly led me into his office and shut the door. Mr. Parmegan was trimly and expensively dressed, as usual, but I was surprised to see both Lamar and Detective Jarvis on hand too.

Mr. Parmegan tried to look superior and officious, as he usually did while talking to me, but worry had turned down the corners of his mouth and wrinkled his forehead, so his expression was nothing more than pitiful.

"Miss Rafferty," he said, "please take a seat." I had no sooner settled into one of the chairs than he said, "I understand that you overheard part of a conversation between Mr. Devane and . . ."

Jarvis threw Mr. Parmegan a warning look, so he continued by saying, "and someone else."

Did he know where I was when I overheard it? Was he going to ask? I held my breath, but he went right past the question.

"And during this conversation they apparently referred to me?" he added.

I nodded. Uh-oh. The moment had come. Good-bye, job. Good-bye, Ridley Hotel.

"Well?" he asked.

"Well?" I repeated.

His impatient expression was beginning to overtake the worried one. "Miss Rafferty," he said, "I would like you to repeat the exact conversation."

I knew I was fidgeting, but I couldn't help it. As I wrapped my legs around the front legs of the chair, I stammered, "I—I m-might not be able to remember it exactly."

Detective Jarvis rested a hand on my arm, giving me a little pat of encouragement. "Take it easy, Liz," he said.

"Just calm down and tell us as well as you can remember."

I took a deep breath and let it out slowly. That helped. "Okay," I said. "Someone named Frank was talking to somebody he called Al, and he said something like, 'We've got them where we want them.' It had to do with a meeting they'd just held."

"What time was this?" Mr. Parmegan asked. Now he looked a little sick.

"Around two or two-thirty," I said.

He looked even worse, but he managed to say, "Please continue."

I thought a minute and said, "I think that Al asked him if some papers were in order, and Mr. Devane—Frank—that was Mr. Devane, wasn't it?" No one answered, so I shrugged and went on. "Anyhow, Frank got kind of crabby and told Al not to bring it up again. He was afraid they'd be overheard."

I paused and smiled. "Which they were. Isn't that funny?"

No one seemed to appreciate the irony, and Detective Jarvis said, "Go on, Liz," so I did.

"Al was kind of tough," I told them. "He said he wasn't going to let anyone get in his way."

I had to stop to think again, but I remembered, "They were talking about Mr. Yamoto. What did they say he was? Oh, yes. Careful. No, cautious. That's it. Cautious. And intelligent. And rich. All of that. But Mr. Devane thought Mr. Yamoto might hire a private investigator and check out stuff."

Now I was coming to the scary stuff—scary because

Mr. Parmegan wouldn't like it. I couldn't leave it out—not when Detective Jarvis was investigating a murder. I just hoped Mr. Parmegan wouldn't blow a fuse. "Al wasn't worried about Mr. Yamoto," I said. "And he wasn't worried about someone named Logan."

Detective Jarvis made a note. "That was the name you heard?"

"Yes. He said Logan was hooked, thanks to Parmegan."

Mr. Parmegan made the tiniest of groans, but he didn't move.

"That's just about all of it," I said.

"Please tell us everything," Jarvis said quietly. "It's important that you tell us every word you can remember."

I stared out the window, wondering why, of all things, I could remember the worst part of the conversation so clearly. I couldn't meet anyone's eyes as I told them, "Mr. Devane said 'you catch big fish if you've got the right bait. I had a hunch Parmegan would make good bait.' And that's it. A busboy came into the room to collect dirty dishes, and the men left."

Mr. Parmegan's face was red, but he turned to me and said, "Thank you for your cooperation, Miss Rafferty. I have one question. How did you happen to overhear this conversation? Where were you at the time?"

It's a good thing I paused, trying to think of the right way to answer, because Detective Jarvis said, "I'm sorry, Mr. Parmegan, but I'm asking Liz not to divulge that information at this time, since knowledge of her whereabouts might be detrimental to the solution of this case."

Wow! That sounded so official, even Mr. Parmegan was subdued. I hoped that Detective Jarvis could read the message in my eyes and see how grateful I was that he had saved me from losing my job. I was grateful to Lamar, too, because he hadn't said a word.

"Is that all?" I asked, eager to get away from Mr. Parmegan's scrutiny.

"No," Jarvis answered. "One of the men involved in this financial venture asked to speak to Mr. Parmegan, so he arranged for him to come to the office. Do you think you could recognize the voice of the one you called Al?"

"I don't know," I said. "Maybe."

Mr. Parmegan picked up his phone and talked to his secretary for just a second. Then he put down the phone and said, "He's here. He's in the outer office."

"Will you go out and talk with him, please, Mr. Parmegan?"

"I—I'm not sure what I should say." I could see that Mr. Parmegan didn't feel like talking to anyone who had referred to him as bait, and I didn't blame him.

"He came here to talk to you," Jarvis said. "He'll have something to say. Just try to draw him out."

Mr. Parmegan left his office, not closing his door. His voice was still stiff as he said, "You wanted to see me, Mr. Ransome?"

I heard Marie excuse herself and the outer door shut. Mr. Ransome must have moved toward the office, because Mr. Parmegan quickly said, "We can speak right here."

"All right, as long as we can't be overheard." Mr. Ransome paused, and when he spoke he sounded terribly embarrassed. "About my drinking too much last night," he said. "I apologize for my obnoxious behavior."

So Mr. Ransome was the jerk who had made all that noise in the lobby. Apparently no one had notified Mr. Parmegan. I'd never forget that voice. It was Al. Detective Jarvis was watching me, so I nodded emphatically.

"I'm afraid I don't understand," Mr. Parmegan said.

"I went to the bar at seven, and stayed much too long," Mr. Ransome said. "I suppose I had too much to drink, and again I apologize, but I must put in a word of appreciation to the member of your security staff who so kindly escorted me back to my room. Please do relay my thanks."

"I will do so," Mr. Parmegan answered.

Mr. Ransome's voice mellowed, as though he'd added a big dose of artificial sweetener, and he said, "There's another reason why I wanted to see you. Granted, we're all upset by the unfortunate death of Frank Devane, but there's no reason why we have to miss out on the investment opportunities we'd been discussing. I have the necessary information and authority, so I hope you'll agree to attend another meeting."

"I—I'm not so sure another meeting would be advisable," Mr. Parmegan said. "I'm sure that Mr. Yamoto has to get back to Tokyo, and Paul Logan informed me that he has a business meeting Monday in Seattle."

"Have you talked to that detective from homicide? He asked our cooperation in remaining over the weekend. I don't know why, but for some reason he wants to question us."

"The reason is simple enough to understand," Mr. Parmegan said, and his voice grew raspy. "Unfortunately, we have a direct connection to the murder victim."

There was silence for a moment, then Mr. Ransome said, "Let's put that concern aside and get back to the point of this conversation. Will you agree to continue our discussions by attending another meeting?"

Mr. Parmegan hesitated, and I could see Jarvis tense. I knew Jarvis was hoping that Mr. Parmegan would be sensible enough to agree.

"Very well," Mr. Parmegan said. "This afternoon? Around two?"

"Fine. Same room?"

"I believe it's available."

There was some small talk as Mr. Ransome moved away, and I could hear the outer door shut.

Mr. Parmegan returned, and Detective Jarvis stood up, saying, "You handled that very well."

"I didn't know whether to agree to a meeting or not. After what you—and Miss Rafferty—told me, I want nothing more to do with those men." He scowled and asked, "Why do you want them to stay here at the Ridley? Why not just let them leave and be done with them?"

Detective Jarvis didn't answer, and I could see the light dawning in Mr. Parmegan's eyes. He paled and said, "I see. You think one of them might be the murderer!"

As Lamar, Detective Jarvis, and I crossed Mr. Parmegan's outer office, Marie was back at her desk. She picked up the phone, and I heard her say, "Yes, sir. Conference room C. Coffee, soft drinks. Candy bars? I'll take care of it, Mr. Parmegan." She put down the phone, smiled at us, and said, "Mr. Yamoto is quite fond of candy bars."

So was I. I thought how nice it would be to have someone like Mr. Parmegan arrange to have candy bars at hand everywhere I went.

I said good-bye to Lamar, who nodded to Jarvis and me before he strode off toward the elevators. But when I tried to say good-bye to Detective Jarvis he said, "Wait a minute, Liz. There are a couple of things I want to talk to you about."

"Okay," I said, and waited, ready to hear what he had on his mind.

But Jarvis took my elbow and steered me down the

hall toward the elevators. "Tell me why you were fingerprinted," he said.

"It was at school," I told him. "One of those child-protection things a few years ago. Everyone in our school was fingerprinted, and our fingerprints, along with our descriptions, were sent to be filed with the Houston police department."

He nodded. "That answers one question. The other one is this: Why did we find one of your fingerprints on the murder weapon?"

"Th-the paperweight?" I stammered, although I remembered the blood on the paperweight and knew without asking that it was the murder weapon.

Someone squealed loudly, and as we turned from the hallway into the waiting area for the bank of elevators, we walked into a team of sleuths eagerly writing in notepads. Sherlock Holmes was still wearing his deerstalker cap—although this morning he seemed to have put it on backward—and he shouted, "Aha! Didn't I say we should follow her?"

The rest of his team were just as excited.

"Detective Sharp deliberately withheld information!" a woman yelled. "She told us the paperweight had been wiped clean."

"She promised to play fair," a tall, thin man objected. "But it's not fair for the police detective to hide the clues."

"Let's go complain!" a tiny woman with a big voice demanded.

"If you do," I told her, "all the other teams will find out."

They looked at me and at each other. "Why are you telling us this?" Sherlock Holmes asked.

"Because I'm innocent," I said, "and the truth will come out sooner or later. Sooner, I hope."

"They all say they're innocent." The tiny woman actually glared at me. "We don't believe you for a minute."

Detective Jarvis and I looked at each other. "We'd better find Mrs. Duffy," I said.

The only reason the team didn't follow us onto the elevator was that Detective Jarvis threatened to arrest every last one of them. It turned out that Sherlock Holmes was an attorney, and he wanted to argue about it, but Jarvis got the last word by closing the elevator door.

As we rode upward I asked him, "Who else's fingerprints were on the paperweight?"

"No one's," he said. "The paperweight was essentially wiped clean, except for one spot along the edge, where one of your fingerprints stood out clearly. The murderer must have known what parts of the paperweight he touched and made sure those were clean."

"I'm glad you don't think I'm the murderer," I told him. "But what about all those sleuths in the mystery game? They'll all think I'm guilty."

The elevator opened, and I saw we were on the nineteenth floor. "Mrs. Duffy isn't staying on this floor any longer," I said.

"I know," Jarvis said. "I'd like to pay another visit to the original scene of the crime."

I shuddered. "You know it's haunted, don't you?"

He didn't answer as we paused outside the door of room nineteen twenty-seven. Automatically, I reached into the pocket of my shorts and pulled out my two keys. As soon as I saw which one was numbered nineteen twenty-seven, I put it into the lock and opened the door.

When Jarvis didn't move I turned to look at him. Passkey in hand, he stared at me with narrowed eyes. "Where'd you get that key, Liz?" he asked.

"Mrs. Duffy gave it to me," I said. "I just forgot to give it back."

"How long have you had it?"

"Since . . . since Fran and I found the body."

"So you could have had it *before* Devane was murdered."

"No!" I said. "Mrs. Duffy gave it to me and asked me to get her notebook from the scene of the crime. I didn't want to go into that haunted place all by myself, so Fran went with me."

He thought a moment and relaxed, so I guessed he was satisfied, but he mumbled, "Are you sure you aren't the one who's haunting it?"

With all our conversation about that key, I should have immediately given it to him, but I was so nervous about going into that suite that I absentmindedly took the key from the door and dropped it back into my pocket.

The room was so cold that Detective Jarvis fumbled with the air conditioner controls. "Sit down, Liz," he said. "I'm going to call Mrs. Duffy."

I perched on the edge of one of the big sofas, listening for whispers, but the room was silent.

Detective Jarvis picked up the phone and asked the operator to connect him with Mrs. Duffy's room. It took less than a minute to reach her, and she must have agreed to come to room nineteen twenty-seven, because he thanked her and hung up the phone.

Jarvis came over to sit beside me. "The operator asked me to tell you, if I saw you, that your mother telephoned and is trying to reach you. Better call home."

I ran for the phone and dialed. Was someone sick? What had happened?

Mom answered on the first ring. "Sweetheart," she said, "how are you?"

"I'm fine, Mom," I told her. "What's the matter? What happened?"

"Nothing happened here," she said, "but we read in the morning newspaper about that savings-and-loan owner getting killed at the Ridley Hotel. Mary Elizabeth, that doesn't have anything to do with your group, does it?"

"Mom, ours is a make-believe murder to solve."

"But they said the murder took place in your mystery weekend's scene of the crime."

"Kind of a coincidence," I answered.

"You're sure you're not involved?"

"Mom," I said, "I'm not a little kid. You don't need to check up on me all the time."

Indignation crept into her voice. "I don't check up on you all the time!"

"What are you doing now, Mom?"

"This is different," she said.

"Okay," I said. "Just don't ask me lots of questions."

"Fine," she said. "We'll just have a friendly chat." There was only a brief pause before she asked, "Tell me, do you have a nice room? Did you sleep well?"

"Mom—" I began.

Her pace quickened. "Are you eating properly? Balanced meals? You did have salad or vegetables for dinner, didn't you?"

There was a knock on the door, and Jarvis answered it, ushering in Mrs. Duffy.

"Living on junk food will only cause problems—"

"Mom," I mumbled into the phone. "Stop worrying about me. I'm a big girl. Anyhow, I can't talk any longer. I'm working."

"I thought you didn't have to work at the club today," she said.

"I'm working to help people solve a murder," I said.

"Oh," she said, and chuckled. "Of course. That's right. The murder-mystery weekend. Well, have fun, dear."

"I will," I said.

"And be sure not to stay up too late and—"

"Good-bye, Mom," I said, and quickly hung up the receiver.

Mrs. Duffy raised one eyebrow as she greeted me. "Detective Jarvis has told me what happened," she said. "I'll have to think of something to cover it."

"It should be easy," I suggested. "I came up here with Tina Martinez—she's with security—to check out this room because there was a complaint about loud noise and music. That's because of the ghost, you know. Anyway, I picked up the paperweight to see if it really was bronze, and I touched a couple of the other things. That's the truth. That's what happened."

"But we're dealing with fiction, not truth," Mrs. Duffy said. "You wouldn't have been able to check out the scene of the crime *before* the murder took place."

"Ooops!" I said.

"Ooops is right," she told me.

Detective Jarvis and I sat quietly for a moment while Mrs. Duffy wrinkled her forehead and made little mumbling noises as though she were talking to herself. Finally she opened her eyes, smiled, and said, "This is how it happened, Mary Elizabeth. As we informed the mystery sleuths, you came to Edgar Albert Pitts's room, at his request, to bring him the script he had left in the health club. You found his door ajar, and when no one answered your call, you walked into his room and discovered the body. So this is what we'll add: The paperweight was lying beside Pitts's body, and you picked it up and looked at it, noticing the blood. Naturally, you immediately dropped it and ran from the room."

I couldn't help groaning. "That's the way it always happens in detective shows on television. I *hate* it when someone finds a body and picks up the weapon. It makes them look so dumb! Nobody with any sense at all would pick up the murder weapon!"

Mrs. Duffy sighed. "I'm sorry, Liz, but I can't think of any other explanation. Can you?"

I thought hard for a couple of minutes. I really did.

Then I had to give up and admit, "I guess there isn't any other reason for my picking up the paperweight."

"Will you go along with the change of script?" she asked.

"I don't have any other choice," I said.

I must have sounded awfully gloomy, because Mrs. Duffy said, "Mary Elizabeth, I have another idea. After the arrest scene, which takes place after the brunch tomorrow morning, Eileen will introduce the actors. I'll ask her to include you, and we can make a point of telling the audience that we had you play your part under your own name in an attempt to mislead and confuse them."

I had to smile. "Won't all those sleuths get angry if you say you were trying to mislead and confuse them?"

"Of course not," Mrs. Duffy said. "That's why people read mystery novels, to get misled and confused." She turned to Detective Jarvis, and her smile broadened. "Do you ever bring your wife to these things?" she asked.

His jaw dropped open for a second. "These things?" he repeated. "Mrs. Duffy, I'm investigating a murder."

"Oh yes," she said. "I'm getting my make-believe murder and the real murder all mixed up."

He paused a moment and said pointedly, "I'm not married."

It didn't take much of a detective to figure out what Mrs. Duffy was getting at. So . . . Eileen Duffy was interested in Detective Jarvis and must have talked him over with her mother. And Jarvis must be somewhat interested in Eileen to have answered the question.

As Mrs. Duffy smiled sweetly at him, Detective Jarvis's face began to turn red. To cover his embarrassment he abruptly reached into his jacket pocket for his pen, but his hand came out with both the pen and a strip of bent, dark cardboard. He turned the cardboard over, studying it as though wondering where it came from.

"Detective Jarvis!" I nearly shouted as the idea bounced into my brain. "Isn't that the piece of cardboard that Mr. Walters—uh—Burns said was wedged under the door to this suite, holding it open?"

"Yes," he said. "It is."

"Don't you know what that is?" I asked him. "It's the kind of cardboard under a candy bar, inside the wrapper."

He sniffed it and nodded. "That's why I've been smelling chocolate all morning."

I clapped my hands together. "It's a clue!" I yelled. "Remember Mr. Yamoto? He constantly eats candy bars!"

"You think Mr. Yamoto used this?" Detective Jarvis asked.

"Yes!" I said.

But Mrs. Duffy took it from Detective Jarvis's fingers, sniffed it, and shook her head. "It's a clue, all right, but it doesn't lead to Mr. whoever you said. It's one of the clues for our mystery-weekend scene of the crime. It was inside a candy-bar wrapper I had placed in the wastepaper basket by the desk. I retrieved the wrapper from those people from the crime lab, but it just occurs to me that when I laid out the clues again in room nineteen twenty-five and put the candy wrapper in the wastebasket, that the little piece of cardboard was missing. It wasn't that important, so I didn't think anything of it."

I slumped into a chair. So much for that good clue. We weren't any closer to the answer of who killed Frank Devane.

"Tell me about these clues you set up at the crime scene," Jarvis asked Mrs. Duffy as he took the small piece of cardboard from her hand and put it back into his pocket. "It looks as if part of this clue has become one of the clues in the Devane murder."

"How?" I asked.

"The murderer used this to prop open the door—I suspect in order to have the body discovered as soon as possible," he answered. "Maybe there are more of Mrs. Duffy's clues that might tie in."

"There's something else we have to know," I said. "What was Mr. Devane doing in the room after the scene had been shut off to visitors?"

"For that matter, why did the murderer choose this room?" Jarvis asked in turn.

"Maybe he was going to meet someone, and he wanted a *very* private place—a place where no one would interrupt him, and he knew no one would come to this room."

"The perp," Mrs. Duffy said.

"Perp what?" I asked.

"The police call people who commit crimes *perps,*" she said. "That stands for *perpetrator.*"

"Unless we're talking to civilians, who wouldn't know what we meant," Detective Jarvis explained.

"But *I* know," Mrs. Duffy said. "I have to know these things in order to make my mysteries authentic." She smiled charmingly. "You asked about the clues I work out for the scene of the crime. As you well know, a murderer always takes something away from the scene and leaves something behind."

"You mean he leaves the murder weapon and then steals something?" I asked.

"No, it's usually something he's not even aware of. He may leave a personal item that relates directly to him, or it may be a blade of grass or some dirt from his shoes. The things I leave at the scene aren't that hard to spot. Some of them give extra information about the suspects. For example, the business card for Arthur Butler. The sleuths discover, through that card, that he writes plays. Some clues simply place a suspect on the scene. Others tell us where he's been. Occasionally, I use a match cover from another city to give that clue. And once in a while I have a cigarette stubbed out so hard in an ashtray that it's torn to shreds." She looked very pleased with herself as she added, "Did you know that points to a *very* disturbed person—someone who could be so upset he might kill?"

"No," I said, but Detective Jarvis pursed his lips and nodded, looking at Mrs. Duffy with surprise.

"What about the murder weapon for Edgar Albert Pitts?" I asked. "Was that in the room too?"

"I'm afraid so," she answered. "When I came to scout out the hotel a few weeks ago, I took note of those heavy bronze paperweights that are in each of the suites and decided to use one of them as the weapon."

The telephone on the desk rang, and it startled me so much that I jumped. Since I was closest, I answered and handed it to Mrs. Duffy, then moved to one of the sofas so that I'd be out of her way.

Mrs. Duffy put down the receiver and said, "They're going to begin another meeting with the detective in ten minutes. Eileen wants me down there right away with the new information about Mary Elizabeth."

As she went through the door I caught a glimpse of some of the sleuths, who were probably leaving Edgar Albert Pitts's scene of the crime.

One of them saw me. "It's that girl from the health club!" she shouted.

"What's she doing in there?"

"I don't know. Let's find out."

As Mrs. Duffy firmly pulled the door shut behind her, Detective Jarvis looked at his wristwatch and said, "Time for me to go too. I've got an appointment to talk with Mr. Yamoto."

I got to my feet as he did, but he waved me back. "This is private, Liz."

"I wasn't going with you. I just want to find Fran."

"Find him in ten minutes, after that detective meeting gets underway and those people in the hall are out of here," he said.

"Can't you take me through them?"

"I don't have time."

"You mean I have to stay here?"

"That's exactly what I mean. Ten minutes at least. We don't want any more misinformation. Let Eileen—uh—Detective Sharp—have the chance to give her mystery fans the information her mother worked out, so she can resolve the problem about your fingerprints on the paperweight."

I sat down again. I had to. My legs wouldn't hold me up. "How can I stay in this suite with a ghost for a whole, long, ten minutes?" I asked, but Jarvis wasn't sympathetic.

"Surely, you don't believe in ghosts," he said.

Detective Jarvis was a big man, so he couldn't open the door just a crack to get through. As he walked into the hallway, the sleuths who had crowded around the door pushed forward, one of them trying to squeeze past him.

"Move back," Jarvis ordered, but I heard their squeals and squeezed my eyes shut tightly.

"That girl from the health club—is she under arrest?"

"Is it true they found her fingerprints on the murder victim's neck?"

"Does she have a record?"

"Is she a member of the Mafia?"

"Has she ever lived in Brazil?"

"Does she like chocolate?"

Detective Jarvis's voice boomed out as the door shut. "Detective Sharp has called a meeting downstairs in the ballroom, and you're all going to miss it! Get out of here!"

The noises ceased, and I leaned back in the sofa, resting my head against its comfortable cushions. I opened my eyes to look at my watch, but from the corner of my eye I caught a slight movement. I jerked to attention, ready to run, but the man who sat on the chair at the desk looked so mournful that instead of being afraid of him, I felt sorry for him. I did wonder, though, how he'd managed to sneak past Detective Jarvis.

The man was neatly dressed in a sport shirt and slacks, and I guessed he was probably somewhere in his late twenties or early thirties. He wasn't looking at me. He just sat with his elbows on his knees, his clasped hands propping up his chin, and his gaze was fixed on the spot where the real murder had taken place.

"Tired?" I asked, and the poor guy looked even droopier.

"All of you are working so hard, trying to solve the mystery." I remembered what Mrs. Duffy had said and told him, "The detective's called a meeting that's going to start in about six or seven minutes. You'd better get down there with your team or you're going to miss all the new information."

He slowly raised his head and began to turn toward me.

"You're not supposed to be in here, you know," I warned him. "And don't expect me to give you any special information, because I won't."

He picked up the telephone, which seemed to detach itself from its cord, and stared right at me with eyes like dark, hollow tunnels. Even though I was terrified, I couldn't look away. A horrible, cold wind wrapped around me, shaking me violently, then freezing me into an ice cube that couldn't move.

I knew without a doubt that this man was the ghost!

Someone should have warned me that the ghost was not a woman wearing a flowing gown and carrying a candle, but a man in torment. I struggled to scream, but my voice twisted into a hard lump, blocking my throat, so I wasn't able to make a sound; and as the man stood and slowly moved toward me, the tunnels in his eyes grew into a black, swirling pit. The pit stretched wider and deeper, and I knew I was going to be sucked inside.

His lips moved, and the whisper came, swirling around inside my head: "Don't leave me."

My head began to pound, and I instinctively clapped my hands over my ears. To my amazement I realized that I could move again, and the ghost had disappeared. The pounding continued, but it was only someone knocking at the door.

"Liz? Are you there?"

Grateful to hear Fran's voice, I ran, stumbling and banging into the furniture and walls, until I reached the door and threw it open. I flung my arms around Fran with such force, I knocked us both off our feet.

"I know you're glad to see me, but greetings like this are hard on my back," Fran mumbled from beneath me.

"Oh, Fran," I cried as I rolled to one side, whacking my elbow in the process, "I saw the ghost!" I sat there shivering and rubbing my aching funny bone while Fran struggled to a sitting position and jerked his rumpled room-service coat back into place.

"A ghost?" Fran tried not to smile as he asked, "What did the ghost do? Moan and rattle chains?"

"I'm not kidding," I told him. "The ghost was a man with pale hair and horrible, terrible, deep black eyes."

"Are you sure it wasn't my math teacher?"

"Be serious," I said. "You can't imagine how awful it was being frozen by a ghost who came at me with a telephone. His eyes grew bigger and bigger until—"

Fran struggled to keep a straight face. "What was he going to do when he reached you? Ask you to make a long-distance call for him?"

"No," I answered, hurt that he wouldn't believe me. "I think he was going to swallow me."

Fran burst out laughing, which really made me angry. "You've got to stop watching Saturday morning cartoons on television," he said.

"Don't be a nerd! It isn't funny!" I snapped. I tried to stay cool, but the memory of that ghost haunted me, and I shuddered right down to my toes.

Fran studied me for a moment, then began to look serious. "You're really scared, aren't you, Liz?" he asked.

"I'm petrified!"

"You actually think you saw someone in that room."

"I *know* I saw someone."

He got to his feet and helped me to get up. "Well, you're not the only one who thinks that room is haunted," he said, "so the best thing to do is stay away from it. Come on. Let's go down to the employees' cafeteria and see if they've got anything edible. We'll have an early lunch."

Fran didn't know it, but what he'd just said had given me a good idea. The ghost was still in my mind, and I had to get help from someone who also believed in him. "First, I want to find Tina," I said. "I need to ask her something."

Fran is a really special person. Even though his stomach was rumbling with hunger loudly enough for me to hear it, he nodded agreement and said, "Tina was in the lobby a few minutes ago. I'll help you find her, and we'll eat later."

We took the elevator down to the first level and had to pass the ballroom. The doors were wide open, and I could hear Detective Sharp quizzing Randolph, who seemed a little nervous. Of course, being Randolph, a murder suspect, he was supposed to be. Fran and I paused to listen in.

"Why did you write that threatening letter to Mr. Pitts?" Detective Sharp asked.

"I had to write," Randolph said. "I kept getting a busy signal when I tried to call him."

"How did Pitts respond when he read the letter?"

"Rudely. He crumpled it into a ball and threw it at me, so I left."

"There's something I don't understand. Why did you walk away and leave that incriminating letter on the floor? Why didn't you pick it up and take it with you?"

Randolph looked puzzled. "I didn't need to," he said. "I already read it."

As the audience laughed, I looked around the room. My attention was suddenly caught by a seedy-looking bum in tattered clothing and a dirty knit cap who was seated near the door, his glance darting from one side to the other.

I grabbed Fran's arm and whispered, "Fran! I think that's a hit man."

"Uh-uh," Fran whispered back. "That's the plain-clothes cop. I saw him showing his badge to Lamar. They must have pulled him in from a stakeout in a downtown alley before he had time to change."

Near the officer sat a woman wrapped in a black cape with dark mascara circles under her eyes, a kid wearing wire spring antennas with revolving eyes on the ends, and the guy in the Sherlock Holmes hat who was chewing on his empty pipe. The cop didn't look any weirder than some of the sleuths.

We walked on, across the lobby, and found Tina near the front desk. She grinned at me and teased, "We all know your fingerprints were on the weapon. It looks pretty bad for you, Liz."

"Forget that mystery-weekend stuff," I said. "Can you come with us to the health club for a minute? I need your help."

"Sure," she said. She gave her location to someone on the other end of her walkie-talkie and followed Fran and me down the hallway. We picked out a table in the far corner, away from the pool, and as soon as we were seated I begged, "Tina, you've got to tell me everything you know about ghosts."

Tina looked so startled that Fran explained, "Liz saw the ghost in room nineteen twenty-seven, and she's kind of shaken up."

"You really *saw* the ghost?" Tina clasped her hands together and her eyes shone. "People have complained about the noise and about the cold in the room, and a few people have heard a kind of whisper—"

"Like us," I said.

Tina looked a little embarrassed. She ignored my remark and finished her sentence. "But nobody's ever really seen the ghost. Tell me about her. Everything."

"It's not a her, it's a him," I said and went on to describe everything that had happened.

"Wonderful," Tina said. "A true manifestation. It can't happen to just anybody, you know."

"It can't?"

"No. Only to those with a certain kind of mind."

"If you're going to say—"

"Receptive," she interrupted. "I was going to say *receptive.*"

"What I need to know is, why did the ghost appear to me? What did he want me to do? And why was he carrying a telephone?"

Tina raised her chin so that she was looking down her nose, which gave her an all-knowing look. She probably practiced that look in front of a mirror. "The telephone is an obvious symbol," she said. "It stands for communication. He was telling you that he wanted to communicate with you."

"Why? He can talk. Wouldn't that be easier?"

"That depends. Did you speak to him?"

"Not after I found out he was a ghost. I was too frightened. Besides, he froze me, so I couldn't move or talk."

"Hmmm," Tina said aloud to herself. "He froze you. I wonder what his purpose was."

"To swallow me?" I suggested.

"An interesting interpretation, but I doubt that it's valid," she said. "Let's forget about the telephone. Let's try to analyze this fixation of yours that the ghost wanted to swallow you."

"It's not a fixation," Fran said helpfully. "It comes from watching too many Saturday morning cartoons."

Tina ignored him. "The fixation stems from a lack of self-worth," she said. "Let's take it step by step. What happens to someone who is swallowed?"

"Well," I said, "she'd fall down a throat and through an esophagus, and end up in a stomach full of acid, and then—"

"Oh, yuck!" Tina said, and looked as though she were going to gag. "That's not what I meant. I'm talking about disappearing. A person who is swallowed would disappear."

"To other people," Fran said. "Not to the person who is swallowed."

"That's beside the point," Tina said. "We're talking about swallowing equaling disappearing equaling a total lack of self-worth."

"Are you saying I *want* to disappear?" I asked her.

"It's my guess," she said, "but tell you what—after I get my degree in psychology, I'll give you a definite answer."

"I can't wait that long," I complained.

The door to the health club opened, and Eileen and Detective Jarvis came into the room. They kept their eyes on each other as they chose a table nearest to the door, so they didn't see us. Eileen glided into a chair and leaned toward Jarvis in a graceful arch, her hair falling gently around her shoulders. Even in that trench coat and fedora she looked like she was posing for a cosmetics ad. Why couldn't I move the way she did?

Detective Jarvis leaned toward her too. Their faces were so close that they could have been discussing top-secret information, but I didn't think that was it.

I wondered if I could rest gracefully in my chair the way Eileen did in hers. If I shifted my legs to the right, crossing one thigh over the other, then leaned forward . . .

Out of balance I grabbed at the table and nearly took it over, too, as my chair went down.

"What happened?" Tina asked, but Fran simply reached down and helped me to my feet.

"I'm clumsy, okay?" I muttered.

Detective Jarvis and Eileen had turned to see what the noise was all about. My face was hot with embarrassment, but I remembered to thank Tina for her help, grabbed Fran's hand, and practically ran out of the health club, not looking at or speaking to anyone else.

"Tina wasn't much help," Fran said, once we had reached the lobby. He added hopefully, "The sleuths are eating lunch. Are you getting hungry yet?"

"I'm starving," I told him. "Do you think the employees' cafeteria has pizza?"

"We can hope," Fran told me.

We weren't in luck. The cook must have been talking to my mother, because there were lots of salads and vegetables—some of them green but undefinable—and the entree was a choice of fried fish, macaroni and cheese, or a brown goop with chunks of things sticking out of it.

"This place makes our school cafeteria look good," Fran said as we took the dishes that seemed most edible and found a table in the crowded room.

He took a large bite of fruit cocktail and told me, "Don't pay any attention to what Tina said. She doesn't know what she's talking about. You don't want to disappear."

Fran had a neat way of making me feel better, and I was awfully glad I was with him. "Not when I'm with you," I said, and gave him a smile.

He smiled back, which wasn't such a good idea, because he'd just taken a bite of the brown goop.

I glanced down at my plate, and remembering my less than graceful attempt to imitate Eileen Duffy, said, "Tina may have been sort of right about my lack of self-esteem, but she doesn't know enough about ghosts. I need to talk to someone who really knows a lot about them."

"Why?" Fran asked.

"Because," I said, and I felt kind of scared putting my thoughts into words, "yesterday a man was murdered in that room, and—think about it, Fran—there was probably only one eyewitness to the crime."

Fran stopped eating. "Who?" he asked.

"The ghost," I said.

Fran took another slow bite. "In that case, you could talk to Mrs. Duffy. A lot of her stories have ghosts in them."

"But Mrs. Duffy doesn't believe in ghosts."

"That doesn't matter. She said she does research on everything she puts into her books, so that means she must do research on the ghosts she puts into them too."

"Maybe you're right." I began to get excited. "I'll talk to Mrs. Duffy as soon as I get a chance."

I found that if I ate fast, I didn't mind the taste so much, so I was through with lunch and eager to go before Fran had finished, and he was very nice about it when I kept telling him to hurry.

A few minutes later we left the cafeteria and went to the house phones, which were near the operator's station in the room behind the desk. As someone walked through the door I heard an operator say, "I'm sorry, sir, we can't give out room numbers, but I'll be happy to connect you with Mr. Jones's room."

I didn't know Mrs. Duffy's room number, but I'd just learned that operators wouldn't give them out, so when I picked up the house phone and an operator answered, I said, "Will you please connect me with Mrs. Roberta Kingston Duffy's room?"

"Thank you," the operator said, and I heard the phone ringing.

Eileen answered, and when I told her who it was she said, "Hi, Liz. What can I do for you?"

I hadn't spoken to her in the health club. I'd been too embarrassed, and I was embarrassed now, but some kind of apology was in order, so I said, "I guess you think I'm kind of a klutz."

"Of course not," she said. "I understand what it's like suddenly to grow tall. I did the same thing."

"But not like me."

"Exactly like you."

It was almost impossible to believe. "My friend, Tina, said I'm clumsy because of my low self-esteem," I told her.

"That could have something to do with it, all right," Eileen said.

I groaned in discouragement, but she told me, "There's an answer, you know, and when we get a chance I'll give it to you."

"Really?"

"Really. I've got to go downstairs now," she added, "so I'll see you later."

"Is your mother there?" I asked quickly. "I need to talk to her."

Eileen was suddenly cautious. "Is this an emergency? Have you said or done something we should know about?"

"No, no. Nothing like that," I assured her. "I just need to ask your mother some questions."

Mrs. Duffy came on the phone, gave me her room number, and invited Fran and me to come right up, so we did.

The Duffys' room wasn't anything like the suite they'd started out with, but it was large and roomy. There was a grouping of two chairs and a love seat next to the window, and we settled there. Mrs. Duffy brought out two cans of cola and invited us to help ourselves from a large container of chocolate brownies.

"Eileen always brings emergency food for her actors," she said. "They work awfully hard, and it makes them hungry."

The way Fran attacked the brownies, I wasn't too sure there'd be any left for the actors, but I had more important things on my mind. "You said you don't believe in ghosts," I told her.

"That's correct."

"But you write about them."

"People like to read about ghosts," she said, "and besides, writing scary scenes is fun."

We were coming to the most important question, and I took a deep breath. "All the things that ghosts do and the way they act—do you just make it all up?"

"I make up what happens in my own stories," she said, "but I base the ghosts' actions on what I've learned about preternatural beings."

"You research ghosts!" I was getting excited.

"That's right."

"Then tell me, please. Do you know how to talk with a ghost and at the same time keep him from swal . . . from harming you?"

Mrs. Duffy leaned back against her chair and smiled. "*If* there were ghosts, you'd have nothing to fear from them," she said. "A ghost can't harm you. It isn't possible, because you have a physical body, and a ghost hasn't."

I shook my head, dissatisfied. "Let me give you an example," I said. "A ghost is in the room with someone, and he freezes her so that she can't move and then comes toward her."

"She freezes herself—with fear," Mrs. Duffy answered.

"No! His eyes freeze her. She looks into them and

sees these horrible black pits, and the black pits grow bigger and bigger . . ." I stopped and shivered as I remembered the ghost and his horrible eyes.

"That's where the girl in your example went wrong," Mrs. Duffy said. "She did freeze herself with her own fear. That's without question. But she *never* should have looked the ghost in the eyes. All the responsible authorities on preternatural affairs are adamant about this. Never ever look a ghost in the eyes."

I practically fell back against the love seat as I let out a long breath of relief.

"You did say she was alone, didn't you?" Mrs. Duffy asked.

"She was alone. Was there something wrong with that?"

"Oh, no. There was nothing wrong—that is, if she wanted to see the manifestation of a ghost. It probably wouldn't have shown up if there was anyone with her. From what I've read, they're inclined to appear to only one person, sort of a one-on-one kind of thing. They aren't fond of groups."

I slid a glance at Fran. "How about two people?"

"It cuts the chances considerably," Mrs. Duffy said.

"One thing about ghosts I don't understand," Fran said. "Why do they hang around?"

"According to authorities," Mrs. Duffy explained, "it's because they haven't come to a complete ending to their lives. They think they can't leave this earth until a wrong has been righted."

"Weird," Fran said, but I could understand how a

ghost would feel. If you'd been suddenly murdered, you would kind of wonder what happened next.

Mrs. Duffy suddenly startled me by saying, "Now that we've finished with hypothetical questions, Mary Elizabeth, why don't you tell me all about your experience with the ghost in room nineteen twenty-seven?"

The phone interrupted, and Mrs. Duffy took the call. As she put down the receiver she said, "You'll have to tell me some other time, Mary Elizabeth. There are a number of sleuths in the health club who want to question you, and Eileen asked if you could get down there as quickly as possible."

We thanked Mrs. Duffy and left her counting the brownies Fran hadn't eaten. I could hardly wait until we were out in the hall before I grabbed Fran's hand and said, "We've got to find Detective Jarvis! Now that we know how to talk to a ghost, he can question the ghost and find out who killed Mr. Devane!"

Fran shook his head and frowned, and I insisted, "Don't you see? The ghost's an eyewitness!"

"Do you really think that Detective Jarvis is going to take your suggestion and go into the real scene of the crime to talk to a ghost?"

"Well," I said, my excitement ebbing away, "maybe I could talk him into it."

"Sure," Fran said. He pressed the elevator button and turned to me. "What's he going to tell his captain? And the district attorney? 'I arrested this guy for murder because a ghost saw the whole thing and ratted on him'?"

Fran was right. I leaned against the wall, wishing the

elevator would hurry and come. "Darn!" I said. "I thought it was such a good idea."

"It is, in a way," Fran said. "If you could tell Detective Jarvis the name of the murderer, he could at least center his investigation on him and maybe find the evidence that would point to his guilt."

"Yes," I said, beginning to feel hopeful again. But something Fran had said suddenly struck me, and I asked, "What do you mean, if *I* could tell Detective Jarvis?"

"Face facts, Liz," Fran said. "No one else has ever seen the ghost. If anyone's going to question him, it will have to be you."

12

I couldn't face that ghost again! I absolutely couldn't! Even if we *never* found out who committed the murder! I answered the sleuths' questions as well as I could and showed them around the health club, as I was supposed to do; but my mind kept going back to the ghost, and I knew I must seem distracted.

Mrs. Bandini and Mrs. Larabee pulled me aside, after the rest of their team had left.

"Did you do it?" Mrs. Bandini asked.

"Do what?"

"Commit the murder," Mrs. Larabee said, and threw an impatient glance at her friend. "You're supposed to say it the right way, like the police do."

"How do you know so much about what the police do?" Mrs. Bandini shot back.

Mrs. Larabee looked smug. "My hairdresser's cousin is married to a security guard."

Mrs. Bandini, somewhat deflated, turned back to me. "Well, did you?" she asked.

"Nobody's supposed to know until the arrest takes place tomorrow at brunch," I said. "But I'll tell you, if you won't tell anyone."

They waited with wide eyes, and they looked as though they weren't breathing.

"I didn't commit the murder," I whispered. "It was somebody else."

"Then why are you looking so guilty?" Mrs. Larabee challenged. "It's confusing everybody."

"I didn't know I was looking guilty."

"Of course you are. A person asks you a simple question and you stare off into space, and sometimes you kind of jump and look behind you. I mean, your behavior is definitely suspicious."

"Oh dear," I said. "I'm sorry. I have something on my mind, and it's a real problem, but it's not Mr. Pitts's murder."

"There, there," Mrs. Bandini said, and she gave me a grandmotherly hug. "We're sorry you have a problem, and no matter what Opal has told you, there is nothing to apologize for. You are a lovely red herring."

"Thank you," I said. Another team was approaching, and I steeled myself to keep my mind on what I was doing. I couldn't ruin the Duffys' mystery weekend.

The sleuths, who had to come up with the answer of who committed Pitts's murder and why before midnight, grew relentless. They dropped any attempts at politeness and grilled me unmercifully, asking so many questions my head began to ache. How could they possibly solve the make-believe murder by discovering whether or not any of the suspects had left a Continental Airlines flight schedule in the dressing rooms? Or the color of the bathing suit Crystal Crane wore in the hot tub? Or if Randolph Hamilton ever mentioned being on a cottage cheese and cucumber diet?

And how could anyone ever solve Frank Devane's murder by refusing to interrogate the only eyewitness?

Filled with guilt by refusing even to consider going back to room nineteen twenty-seven, I went to the last detective's meeting of the day, intending to sit in the back row and listen to the actors and not think a single thought.

As I entered the lobby the crowd had thinned, most of them hurrying to the ballroom to get the best seats. Randolph, in conversation with Crystal, was crossing the lobby from the left, but a nondescript man in a dull-looking suit made a beeline toward them from the right. He strode steadily and quickly, and as he approached he slipped his right hand under his open suit jacket and began to withdraw it with something in it. Without stopping to think I ran toward Randolph, not too sure what was happening yet aware that something was not what it should be.

I saw the man's hand emerging, the shine of metal, and—with a yell—I flung myself at Randolph and Crystal, knocking them to the ground and landing on top of them.

I wasn't the only one yelling. Footsteps pounded past my head, a gun slammed onto the carpeting near my nose, and something went over with a crash.

"It's okay, Liz. Everything's okay. Stop screaming," I

heard Detective Jarvis say. His hands gripped my shoulders, and he lifted me to my feet.

I dusted myself off and saw that Randolph and Crystal were standing, with no bones broken, Detective Jarvis was now holding the gun, and the officer in the weird clothes had handcuffed the man in the suit and was leading him out of the hotel, accompanied by a couple of uniformed officers who had appeared from nowhere.

"Did that girl try to kill Randolph?" A woman pointed at me.

"No," Jarvis said. "Liz saved his life."

Mrs. Bandini beamed at me proudly, but Sherlock Holmes scowled at Jarvis and asked, "Just who are you?"

"I'm a detective from homicide," Jarvis said.

Eileen made her way through the crowd, and Mrs. Larabee said loudly, "Are you Detective Sharp's partner? Is that right?"

"That's right," Eileen said and gave Jarvis a wink as she stepped to his side. "I'm going to ask Detective Jarvis to tell you what happened. Then we can all go back into the ballroom for our predinner meeting. Some more information has come in regarding our suspects."

"Like what?" a man asked.

"You'll find out when the meeting begins," Eileen told him.

Sherlock Holmes interrupted. "I'd like to know if Martin Jones has put any money into one of those offshore banks in the Cayman Islands."

That was a weird question. Maybe Sherlock had been reading about that big trial and that's why the Cayman Island banks had come into his mind. Or maybe Mrs. Duffy had put something about the banks into her plot. I hadn't been following the story, so I didn't know.

Eileen's expression showed that she was surprised too. "As a matter of fact, I'll be able to give you that information," she said.

Sherlock turned to one of his teammates and mumbled, "Aha! Laundering money! What did I tell you?"

Eileen said a quick word to Detective Jarvis, who nodded agreement. He looked very uncomfortable as he faced the group, but he said, "Ladies and gentlemen, you want to know what happened here. Okay. The man who was wearing the knit cap was one of our undercover officers who was on stakeout here at the hotel."

"That was a stupid outfit for a plainclothes officer to wear to the Ridley," Sherlock said loudly. "He looked like he belonged in an alley."

"Oh, be quiet!" Mrs. Larabee told him. "I liked the actor's costume. He looked cute."

"Actor," Jarvis said. "Uh—yes, actor. The other actor was a known hit man. He was—uh—after Randolph Hamilton, who had borrowed money from the wrong kind of lending agency and hadn't repaid it."

"Oooh! New information!" someone cried, and a number of the sleuths began scribbling in their notebooks.

The tiny woman I'd seen before called out in a loud voice. "Are you telling us there were *two* gamblers? It's already been established that Martin Jones gambles, and now you're saying that Randolph Hamilton gambles too."

Eileen gave her mother a frantic look, but Mrs. Duffy nodded and smiled. I guess having two gamblers wouldn't hurt the script. Jarvis went on as though he were an actor himself. "That's what I'm saying."

"Then there could be collusion!" Excitement kept her from whispering to her teammates, so everyone in earshot made further notes.

"Pay attention, please," Jarvis told them. "Our plain-clothes detective had a make on the hit man and was approaching. However, the hit man pulled a gun, Mary Elizabeth Rafferty saw it, and she pushed Randolph and Crystal Crane out of the way."

"Isn't she a sweet, darling girl?" Mrs. Bandini said.

I heard Sherlock mumble to the man next to him, "Think about it, Randolph can't pay his gambling debts, but Martin Jones can. Where does Jones get the money?"

Randolph spoke up, his voice so shaky he could hardly talk. "Believe me, I'm very grateful to you, Miss Rafferty!" he said, and tears spilled down his cheeks.

"Awwww." The audience let out a collective, sympathetic sigh, and I heard someone murmur, "Scratch Randolph Hamilton as murderer. He couldn't have done it."

Eileen took command. "Thank you for your report, Detective Jarvis," she said as she briskly stepped forward. "Come on now, everyone. Back to the ballroom. I'll give you the rest of the evidence that has turned up."

As she passed me she surreptitiously took my hand and squeezed it, which made me feel good. While everything was happening I didn't have time to think about it. I'd just reacted. But now it was all sinking in. I had saved Randolph's life. In spite of all the klutzy goofing-up I'd been doing, I'd actually done something right.

Randolph paused to give me a quick one-armed hug, which was fine, except that he was blowing his nose into a large handkerchief at the same time.

He hurried after the others, and only Detective Jarvis, Mrs. Duffy, and I were left.

"What's going to happen to Randolph?" I asked Jarvis. "They'll send another hit man after him, won't they?"

Mrs. Duffy answered first. "After lunch Eileen and her actors held a meeting. We decided to pool our resources and pay off Randolph's—uh—John's debt, and he's promised to pay us back and join Gamblers Anonymous and never gamble again."

"That's very nice of you," I told her. "I've got a couple of dollars I could contribute, if that would help."

"Every little bit will help," she said. "How that man could run up such a large debt . . ."

I turned to Detective Jarvis, determined that I was going to keep on doing the right things. "I need to talk to you," I told him.

"Come with me," he said. "I have a phone call to make."

We left Mrs. Duffy and went to a small office that

apparently had been given to Detective Jarvis for his own use.

"Sit down," he said, so I sat at the table and studied the small computer and the fax machine while he made a call. I'd never used a fax machine, and I wondered if anybody would care if I faxed something to someone. I gave up the thought, because I didn't know anyone who had a fax machine, so there'd be no one to fax anything to even if I could think of something to fax.

While I sat there I couldn't help overhearing Jarvis's conversation, so I knew he was talking to someone downtown at police headquarters.

"According to Parmegan's account of the meeting this afternoon, Ransome wanted the other investors to stay in the deal, but they're all wary now. It sounds like another land-flip fraud."

He listened a moment, then said, "I talked to each of them alone. In my opinion Yamoto, Logan, and Parmegan are innocent dupes. None of them had a reason to murder Devane. Have you got anything yet on Ransome?"

Again he listened and gave a low whistle. "Some of these guys thought savings and loans were set up for their own benefit," he grumbled. "Okay, so Ransome is as guilty of fraud as Devane, but at the moment I can't see any motive for murder here. On the contrary, a bunch of pigeons are flying right out of his grasp. If Devane hadn't been murdered they probably would have pulled off this scheme without a problem."

Again he listened and made some notations in his

notebook. "Yeah, swampland," he said. "Not hard to guess."

In a few moments he had finished his conversation and turned to me. "Okay, Liz, let's hear it from the top."

"That's the way actors talk," I told him. I'd heard Eileen say that.

His face got a little red, and he said, "I've been talking to actors. Maybe I picked it up from them." He shifted in his chair and looked at his watch. "What was it you wanted to see me about?"

"Could I tell you something important about the ghost in room nineteen twenty-seven?"

"No," he said. "I haven't time. I want to try to clear up this murder before the weekend is over and everyone lights out. I can't keep them all here much longer."

"But the ghost can tell you who committed the murder. The ghost is the only eyewitness."

"Fine," he said, with more than a hint of sarcasm—which I didn't appreciate—and adjusted his pen so the tip came out. "Now, let's get down to business."

But I wasn't through with my questions. "What happened to him?" I asked.

"What happened to who?"

"The guy who got killed in room nineteen twenty-seven a couple of years ago. You've been in homicide for longer than that. Do you remember the case?"

Jarvis nodded. "His name was Larry . . . Larry something, and he and his wife had been arguing."

Larry. I liked knowing his name. It made him just a little bit less scary than when he was nameless. Of course, his name could have been something weird, like Vladimir or Freddy. "What was Larry's wife's name?" I asked.

Jarvis thought just a moment. "Linda. That's it. Larry and Linda. Anyway, Linda lost her temper and hit Larry over the head with a large vase, I think. She hit him too hard, and as a result, was tried on a charge of voluntary manslaughter and convicted."

"What happened to her?"

"She's in a women's correctional institution near Digby, just north of Houston." Not even trying to disguise his impatience, Detective Jarvis said firmly, "That's enough, Liz. We haven't got time to digress anymore. I want you to tell me as carefully as you can what you saw in the lobby, starting with just before you spotted the man who was going after Randolph Hamilton."

I told Jarvis my story over and over again. I hate the way detectives ask questions. They want to know every little tiny exact detail, and I didn't think what had happened in the lobby was nearly as important as trying to find out who killed Frank Devane.

Finally Jarvis seemed satisfied, and he told me I could go. I hurried out into the hallway, desperate to find Fran. Where was he? I needed him.

"Hi," Fran said behind me, making me jump a foot in the air. "What's going on?"

I turned and grabbed his shoulders. "Fran! Where have you been?"

"In my room," he said. "It wore me out to answer so many questions, especially since I didn't know the answers to most of them, so when I got a chance I sneaked upstairs for a minute and kind of fell asleep. Did anything happen while I was gone?"

"I saved Randolph from a hit man."

"Good for you," he said. "What else is new?"

There was no point in trying to explain. Fran would find out the story soon enough. "You were right about one thing," I admitted. "I told Detective Jarvis about the ghost being an eyewitness to the murder, and he wasn't the least bit interested."

"I won't say 'I told you so,' " Fran said.

"Thanks. I appreciate that." I took a long breath, tried to steady myself, and said, "I really don't have a choice, Fran. I've got to go back and talk to that ghost."

Fran groaned and said, "In a way, I wish you wouldn't."

I melted. Good old Fran. Who could be nicer? Who could care more about me?

"Because if you do, I know you're going to make me go with you," Fran added.

I gave him a look of total disgust, but he didn't seem to catch it. "This is something I have to do alone," I said. "I'm the only one the ghost has ever appeared to, and he may not show up if anyone's with me."

"Oh, well, in that case," Fran began.

I started to get mad at him, but he burst out laughing, so I knew he'd been teasing me all along.

"You really do care what happens to me," I said.

"You bet I do," Fran answered, and he grew more serious. "Liz, don't jump at this thing too fast. When Detective Jarvis gets all the facts together, he'll solve the case, and there probably won't be any reason for you to have anything to do with that ghost."

I was insistent. "Fran, there aren't enough facts to

help Jarvis solve this case, but the ghost saw whoever it was who murdered Frank Devane. What else is there to think about?"

"Come on," he said and took my hand. "Let's find some quiet place and talk about it."

"Not an empty conference room with leftover food in it."

He paused. "Okay. We'll do it your way. Let's go to the health club."

As we sat again at the far end of the room, Fran said, "Let's go about this in an orderly way. The first thing to do is list the murder suspects."

I sighed. "That's the trouble. There aren't any, except for Mr. Burns, and Detective Jarvis thinks he was telling the truth and didn't commit the murder."

"How about Al—Albert Ransome, who helped Devane set up the meeting to fleece investors?"

"I heard Jarvis tell someone at headquarters that Ransome doesn't have a motive, that he'd probably be better off financially if Devane hadn't died and they'd have been able to hold the meeting the way they'd planned it. Jarvis doesn't think Ransome's involved in the murder."

"What about the others in that financial thing?"

I shook my head. "He said they were innocent dupes."

Fran had to smile at that. "I like thinking of our esteemed hotel manager as a dope—uh—dupe."

I heard the buzz of one of the surveillance cameras and saw it turn on us. "Be quiet," I whispered.

"They can see us, but they can't hear what we're saying."

"How do you know they can't read lips?"

"They can't," Fran said. "Now . . . to get back to suspects. What about Mrs. Duffy?"

I made a face at him. "Mrs. Duffy just commits murders on paper."

"Does she?" Fran asked. "She's got all those ideas in her head. What if she decided really to use one of them?"

What he said made me stop and think. "There are some strange coincidences," I admitted. "Mrs. Duffy's victim and the real murder victim were hit on the head, both in the same room. And there must be something in Mrs. Duffy's script about money laundering in the Cayman Island banks, because Sherlock Holmes asked about it, and that's one of the crimes Stephanie Harmon's boss is going on trial for."

"How about Stephanie Harmon?" Fran asked. "She was right next door. She could have killed him."

"No, she couldn't. She's had a police officer with her every minute."

"Every single minute?"

"Well, no," I told him. "I mean, after she goes to bed, or when she takes a bath—stuff like that—she's by herself, but the police officer would see her if she left the room."

"She couldn't sneak out?"

"How?"

"There's a sliding glass door in her bedroom. She

could have gone out on the balcony and over to the sliding glass door in the next suite and let herself in."

"Wrong," I said. "When the police examined the room, after Mr. Devane was murdered, they said the doors to the balcony were locked."

I suddenly sat up straight. "Wait a minute, Fran! The Duffys had put tape across the lock of the door opening into the hallway so that their actors could take a few minutes to go up there and get familiar with the scene of the crime."

"But how would Stephanie Harmon know that?" Fran asked.

The scene came into my mind with a rush. "Randolph was looking for Mrs. Duffy and knocked on the wrong door—Stephanie's door. The policewoman opened it, but Stephanie saw Randolph and screamed."

"She's kind of high-strung. She probably screams at everything."

"Don't distract me," I said. "I was going to tell you that Mrs. Duffy told Randolph he could have gone into the scene of the crime, because they'd put tape across the lock so the actors could get into the room without a key."

"Stephanie could have heard her?"

"Yes."

"Do you think she could have sneaked away from her bodyguard and gone into the room next door?"

I sighed. "I don't see how. Besides, there's still a big, unanswered question, and that is, what was Mr. Devane doing in room nineteen twenty-seven?" An idea began wiggling in my mind, and it started to get close enough so I could almost catch it, but just then Tina came to join us and I lost the thought.

She slid into a chair and said, "I saw you here on the monitor, and I just had to tell you, Liz, that what you did was fantastic."

"Thank you," I said.

"I mean, you risked your life to save Randolph Hamilton's. That was awfully brave of you."

"I really wasn't brave," I said. "I just saw the man coming with a gun and acted without thinking."

Fran's head swiveled back and forth as though Tina and I were playing catch. "Okay," he finally said. "What are we talking about?"

Tina looked surprised. "Liz kept a hit man from killing Randolph. Didn't she tell you?"

"Well, yeah," Fran said, "I guess she did, but . . ."

"It takes you a while to catch on, huh?" Tina asked.

"Aw, come on," Fran mumbled.

Tina giggled. "You could phone in your answer, but you're one number short."

"Oh, yeah," Fran said and grinned. "Well, let me tell you—"

Suddenly the thought in my mind took shape, and I cried out, "Wait a minute! Fran! Tina! Everyone's been talking about phone calls. You, Detective Jarvis, Lamar. Even the ghost was holding a telephone."

Tina put on her authoritative expression and said, "We've already discussed the symbolism in that action."

"What if it wasn't symbolism? What if the ghost was trying to tell me something real?"

"Like what?" Fran asked.

"Like the fact that someone in room nineteen twenty-seven had been using the telephone."

"That's hardly news. Everybody uses the telephone," Tina said.

"But not at the scene of a murder." I got so excited I swung around in my chair and nearly knocked it over. Righting myself I said, "Tina, you know everybody in the hotel. Do you think that the operators would tell you if anyone made a phone call from that room?"

"If a caller was dialing a local or long-distance call, the operators wouldn't know. The call would go through the computer system."

"But it wouldn't if someone were calling someone else in another room and didn't know the number. They'd have to go through the operator. Maybe an operator would remember."

"Operators handle thousands of calls. How would they remember?

"If a celebrity stays in the hotel and calls the operator, the operator would remember, wouldn't she?"

Tina thought a moment. "I don't think we ever had a real celebrity stay here—I mean anyone terribly important, although there once was a country-western singer who brought his horse and—"

"Tina, could you ask the operators for me?"

"Ask them what?"

"If Stephanie Harmon placed any calls to Frank Devane, and if she made any other calls."

"What have you got in mind?"

"The beginning of an idea. I'll tell you about it later, because I might be wrong."

Tina still looked dubious. "If an operator remembers placing the call, she won't be able to tell you what they talked about, because she wouldn't have listened in."

"I know that," I answered. "I just need to find out if a call was made and about what time it was made."

Tina slowly got to her feet, and Fran and I pushed back our chairs and stood too. "I'll do it," she told me, "but I feel kind of stupid about asking, because Lamar told me that Stephanie Harmon recognized Devane but didn't even know his name."

"She screamed at him—or rather, the man she thought was him."

Fran shook his head. "I agree with Tina on this one. Remember when Stephanie arrived at the Ridley? The actors passed her near the service elevators, and she was so nervous she practically passed out. If any of them had spoken to her she probably would have screamed then too."

"I don't think so," I said. "I may be wrong about the call, but we won't know unless Tina at least gives it a try."

"Okay." Tina motioned to us. "Come on. I'll ask right now."

Fran and I had to stand outside the door to the switchboard office and wait, but we didn't have to wait long. Tina came back out in just a few minutes, with a surprised look on her face.

"On Friday evening Bobbie Jean took a call from a woman in room nineteen twenty-seven, who asked to be connected with Frank Devane's room. Bobbie Jean remembered because she knew that nineteen twenty-seven was the crime scene for the mystery weekend."

"Does she know who the woman was?"

"No, and the woman didn't give a name. Bobbie Jean thought she was probably Mrs. Duffy or Eileen Duffy."

"Was Devane in his room? Did he take the call?"

Tina nodded, but she said, "I don't know what that proves, since we don't know who called him."

"The Duffys didn't know him."

"So they said."

"What about calls from nineteen twenty-nine? Stephanie Harmon's room?"

"There's a charge for local and long-distance calls, so they're on the computer, but that's private information. The operators wouldn't give that out."

"What about other calls to rooms in the hotel?" I asked.

"No charge, so no record. You were just lucky that the call you wanted to know about went through an operator and Bobby Jean remembered it."

In my excitement I grabbed Tina's arm. "Bobby Jean told you about the room-to-room call. Don't you think she'd look up the other calls for you?"

"I know she wouldn't, because I already asked. She said she couldn't give me any information about the long-distance call made from nineteen twenty-nine."

So there *was* a long-distance call. I looked at my watch. "It's dinnertime," I told them.

"Good thought," Fran answered enthusiastically.

"Let's get down to the cafeteria before all the good stuff is gone."

"I wasn't thinking about dinner. I was guessing that Officer Maria Estavez ought to be back on duty, and I could talk to her."

"About what?"

Tina's walkie-talkie beeped, and she said, "I've got to get back to the monitor room." She put a hand on my arm, and her eyebrows dipped into a frown. "Liz, talk to Detective Jarvis about whatever you've got in mind. Don't try to figure out all these things by yourself."

I nodded. "He could find out about the long-distance call. Bobbie Jean would tell the police, or else Detective Jarvis could subpoena the records, like Lamar Boudry's friend did."

"What friend?" Tina asked.

"It's a long story. Ask Lamar. He'll tell you."

Tina left, and Fran said, "I agree with Tina on this one too. I don't see how Stephanie could have got away from her bodyguard to murder Devane, but somewhere in this hotel there may be a murderer, and you could be in danger if you get too close to what really happened."

"I just want to make one phone call," I told Fran. "There's something more I have to know."

"Could you wait until *after* dinner?" Fran asked. "I'm getting awfully hungry."

"You're always hungry," I said. "My call won't take long."

"Okay," Fran said with a long, miserable sigh. "Go ahead."

We were close to the house phones, so I picked up the nearest one and asked for room nineteen twenty-nine. On the second ring there was kind of a double click and Officer Estavez answered. I recognized her voice and blurted out, "Hi! This is Mary Elizabeth Rafferty, and you're just the person I want to talk to."

She repeated my name in the vague way people have when they can't remember who you are, so I explained, "I'm the one who found Frank Devane's body."

"Oh," she said. "I remember now. What can I do for you?"

"You can tell me about phone calls from your room," I said.

"There's nothing much to tell about them," she answered, and her voice sounded puzzled. "I've called downtown a couple of times, to report. The other officers do the same."

"I mean Miss Harmon's calls, especially a long-distance call," I said.

"You'd have to discuss that with her. As far as I know, she hasn't made any."

"Would you know if she did? I remember telephones all over that suite—even in the bathroom."

There was silence for a moment before Estavez asked, "What's this all about?"

"I'm not sure yet," I answered.

Her voice became stern. "I hope you're not meddling into police business."

"I was just asking a question," I said.

"If you have any more questions, ask Detective

Jarvis," she told me. "As a matter of fact, I just might ask Detective Jarvis what you think you're doing."

"I'm sorry I bothered you," I said quickly, although I really wasn't. "I won't call you again."

"Don't come up here either," she ordered.

She could keep me away from their room, but surely she couldn't keep me away from the entire nineteenth floor, could she?

"Uh, look," I said, wanting to make sure, "I promise I won't bother you, but I've got to go up to the nineteenth floor because there's something I need to find out at the scene of the murder."

Officer Estavez didn't answer. She didn't even say good-bye. She just hung up, and again, almost immediately, there was a second click. I didn't give any thought to it, but later, oh how I wished I had!

"Now can we eat?" Fran asked in a pitiful voice.

"Fran!" I said, putting my head close to his, so I could keep my voice down. "Listen to what I found out. Stephanie Harmon could have called a thousand people, and her bodyguards wouldn't have known about it."

"What would these thousand people do?"

"Stop being silly, and listen to me. What do you think of this idea? Suppose Stephanie talked a couple of times over the phone to Frank Devane. I *know* she knew him, but she wouldn't admit it, so I bet they were involved in something illegal. Maybe it was some crooked deal Devane had going with her boss. She might have had a part in it too."

"Maybe she was blackmailing Devane," Fran suggested.

"Hmmm, that's not a bad idea," I said. "Anyhow, Stephanie hears Mrs. Duffy say that the room next door is taped open. Stephanie tells Officer Estavez that she's going to take a nap, she waits for her chance, sneaks out of the room and into nineteen twenty-seven. Then she telephones Frank Devane through the operator and asks him to meet her there. He does, and she hits him on the head and kills him." I stepped back and held out my hands. "There. What do you think of that?"

"I don't think she could have got out of the room with the police officer right there."

"Sure, she could. Let's say that she waited for Estavez to go into the bathroom. Then Stephanie could sneak out of her bedroom and out the front door, and her bodyguard would think she was still asleep in the bedroom and wouldn't know the difference."

"How would Stephanie have got back in her own suite without Estavez seeing her?"

"Well," I said. "Well . . . uh . . . I'll think about that part later."

"While we're eating, I hope?" Fran asked.

"Okay," I said, but we didn't have a chance to go down to the dining room.

Mrs. Duffy sailed out of the ballroom in a hurry and stopped, looking around. As she spotted us an expression of joy and relief lighted her face, and she zoomed toward us.

"Mary Elizabeth!" she called, as soon as she was in hearing distance. "We're nearly at the end of the last detective's meeting before we break for dinner, and an important question has come up. Some of the sleuths want to know about the manuscript you found—the one you tried to return to Mr. Pitts."

I shrugged. "There isn't anything to say about it, is there?"

"As a matter of fact, considering the changes we've had to make in the script, I think this would be a good opportunity to strengthen one of the clues." She took my hand and began to lead me back toward the ballroom. "Now, this is what you tell them: The manuscript was fastened inside a navy-blue cardboard folder. It fell open as you picked it up, and you saw the title and name of the author."

I turned, and made a hopeless gesture at Fran. "Go on down to the cafeteria," I called to him. "I'll join you in just a few minutes."

Mrs. Duffy, intent on her script, was going on at full steam. "The title of the play was *Too Late for Darkness,* and the author was Arthur Butler. Can you remember that?"

"*Too Late for Darkness,* Arthur Butler," I repeated.

"Fine," Mrs. Duffy said, and we entered the ballroom.

As one hundred and forty-eight heads turned toward me, I got an inspiration I couldn't ignore.

Fran was occupied, I'd be free from the sleuths in just a few minutes, and this would be the perfect opportunity to visit room nineteen twenty-seven. I was almost positive that Stephanie Harmon had killed Frank

Devane, but I needed more information. I was sure that the ghost—the only eyewitness—had the rest of the answers I needed, and what's more, it dawned on me that I had something important to tell the ghost.

I explained to Detective Pat Sharp what Mrs. Duffy had asked me to say, but I was trapped on the stage while the actors went through their lines. Before I arrived Detective Sharp had divulged the last of the evidence against each of the suspects, so she went into a kind of recap while the actors responded, and I was interested in spite of myself.

"I know it looks bad for me because I was paying blackmail to Mr. Pitts," Annabelle wailed. "But I didn't kill him!"

Detective Sharp turned to Arthur Butler. "We subpoenaed the contents of Edgar Albert Pitts's safe-deposit box, and found in it two copies of the same play —one with your name on it as author, and one with the name of Harvey Hamlick as author. We attempted to contact Mr. Hamlick at the address typed on the manuscript, and discovered that two years ago he disappeared."

Arthur Butler squirmed and muttered, "I don't know

any Harvey Hamlick. I don't know what you're talking about. And furthermore, you're wrong if you're intimating that I killed Edgar Albert Pitts!"

"I talked to a Mr. I. B. Topps, Miss Crystal Crane's agent," Detective Sharp told the audience. "I understand that Mr. Pitts refused to release Miss Crane from her contract with him, which meant she'd miss out on a very good part in a television situation comedy. However, Mr. Topps told me that Miss Crane telephoned him Friday afternoon and told him she'd be able to audition for that part and would soon be free from her contract with Mr. Pitts."

Crystal gasped and actually looked pale. "I could have talked him into releasing me," she cried. "I know I could! So don't ask me if I killed him, because I didn't!"

Detective Sharp consulted her notes and continued. "We checked Mr. Randolph Hamilton's work record, and it seems that over the years he has made more money as a dishwasher than as an actor."

"All right!" Randolph exploded. "I admit Pitts fired me, and we had quite an argument about it, and I lost my temper." He paused and cried out, "Don't look at me like that! I didn't hit him! I didn't kill Edgar Albert Pitts!"

Calmly, Detective Sharp turned a page in her notebook, studied her notes, and said, "Martin Jones, over the years you've asked your uncle for some sizable loans, which he's given you, but apparently, on Friday you asked him to lend you a large amount of money, and he refused, even though you were overheard telling him that you were desperate."

"All right! I was desperate!" Martin shouted. "But that doesn't mean I'd kill my uncle Edgar! I didn't do it!"

Detective Sharp turned to the audience and said, "I think we can examine the evidence we've got and soon come up with the answers. If you think about what you've seen, what you've heard, and what you've learned through interviewing the suspects, you'll have all the clues you'll need to arrive at the solution of this case. Pay particular attention to everything found at the scene of the crime. What was important and what was not? As sleuths, it's up to you to determine what has a bearing on this case.

"It's time for dinner in ballroom B right now, but later you'll still have time to question any of the suspects again or to make another visit to the scene of the crime. Then get together with your team members for a final conference. Make your decision as to who killed Edgar Albert Pitts and why. Turn your cards in to the front desk any time before midnight. They'll be time-stamped, so in case of a tie, the first team to reach the solution will win. Our next meeting will be in ballroom B, tomorrow morning following brunch at nine-thirty, and I hope at that time to be able to make an arrest."

I glimpsed Detective Jarvis at the back of the room, and he didn't look as though he were trying to solve Devane's murder. He had a kind of silly smile on his face as he kept his eyes on Eileen Duffy.

The sleuths slowly got up from their folding chairs and made their way out of ballroom A into ballroom B, talking faster than they were walking. Some of them were so wrapped up in solving the mystery, I think they would have willingly skipped dinner, although the food they were being served was the Ridley chef's finest. As I left the room I caught a fragrant whiff of roast prime rib in its rich, herb-flavored juices, and became so hungry that I nearly postponed what I had to do; but I reminded myself that the employee cafeteria food was not prepared by a chef, and I'd get only macaroni and cheese or some of that brown stuff, and that thought kept me on track.

As I approached the elevators Mrs. Bandini and Mrs. Larabee caught up with me. "Can you come to dinner with us?" Mrs. Bandini asked. "We can grill you while we eat."

I smiled. "You already know everything I know, and I'm not allowed to eat with the mystery-weekend people. I have to eat my meals in the employees' cafeteria."

"Is that where you're going now?" Mrs. Larabee asked.

"Not exactly," I answered. I saw Fran heading toward the ballroom, looking for me. Fortunately, an elevator door opened, and I ducked inside. It was all I could do to keep my courage up. I suspected that Fran might decide to talk me out of visiting the ghost alone, and—as I'd told him—I couldn't allow him to go in the room with me, because I was sure then that the ghost wouldn't appear.

I'd intended a number of times to give back the key to room nineteen twenty-nine, and something had always distracted me, so I still had it in my possession. Maybe it was an omen. Maybe it was supposed to be this way, because now I'd have no problem opening the door.

The nineteenth-floor hallway was quiet as I stepped out of the elevator, and only my double determination kept me from turning around and taking that elevator back downstairs. I was unable to tolerate the heavy silence that pressed against my ears like thick wads of cotton, so I hummed a little to myself as I walked to the door of nineteen twenty-seven, and I deliberately made noise with the key in the lock as I opened the door.

From the corner of my eye I saw the door to room nineteen twenty-nine open just a little. I didn't want to argue with Officer Estavez about whether or not I should be up here, so I quickly went inside nineteen twenty-seven and shut the door tightly behind me.

I didn't turn on the main light switch. The sky was gold with summer's evening sun, and there was enough light through the glass wall in the dining room to illuminate the room. I didn't want to scare away the ghost—Larry—with too much brightness. Having one of us scared to death was enough. My breath came in little gasps, and I wasn't sure my knees would hold me up as I walked into the living room, step by step, and flopped into the nearest chair.

I waited, listening, hoping, watching for some sign of the ghost, but nothing happened. The room was silent and cold—very cold—and once I jumped and cried out as I felt a flutter of air near my right shoulder.

But it was nothing. As patiently as I could, I waited.

Finally, I couldn't stand it any longer. "Larry?" I

whispered in a voice so shaky and rough it sounded as though I were recovering from a bad case of tonsillitis.

The word hung in the air, vibrating, moving. I could see it shiver toward the window, twanging like a harp string; and it began to take shape until it became the ghost I had seen here before.

His back was to me as he leaned against the glass door, his forehead pressing against the glass. Who did he remind me of? Who had I seen in that same position in the same place?

Stephanie Harmon! Of course! The way she had stood at the door after she'd seen Frank Devane's body.

But the ghost . . . what was he doing with his right hand? Opening, then locking the latch on the sliding glass door!

"Stephanie did that, didn't she?" My words were loud in my ears, but I had to communicate with this ghost. "The glass door was unlocked, and she locked it while she stood there. When the policeman checked, he said both doors were locked. But this one hadn't been, had it, because Stephanie had gone through it to reach the unlocked door to her bedroom? It was open until Stephanie locked it!"

As it all came together, the ghost began to turn toward me, and I lowered my eyes to stare down at his feet. "I know now that I'm not supposed to look into your eyes," I said, "so I won't make that mistake again. But I had to come and thank you for your help. I got your message about the telephone, even if you did scare me to death giving it to me. And I understand now how Stephanie got into and out of the room."

The ghost moved closer, but I stood up and didn't flinch. Maybe even when ghosts were trying to be helpful they still had to frighten people. It probably wasn't his fault at all.

I tried to stop shivering as I hugged my shoulders and rubbed my cold arms. "Larry," I said, "I know your name, and I know that you don't need to stay here any longer." He stopped a few feet away from me and sort of floated in space, so I went on. "I think you're still here because you don't know what happened, so I'm going to tell you. Linda was tried and convicted of voluntary manslaughter, and she's serving time right now in a women's correctional institution near Digby. In case you want to visit her, it's just north of Houston."

There was a terrible stir of air, which almost took my breath away, and Larry vanished. It was not only a lot more comfortable without a ghost in the room, but I felt good about releasing him. He'd done a favor for me, and I'd been able to do one for him in return. I just wished he'd taken his cold air with him. Or maybe the freezing temperature in this suite really was the fault of the air conditioner.

While I was smiling to myself, pleased about the way things were turning out, there was a sharp rap on the glass door, and I saw the uniformed sleeve belonging to Officer Maria Estavez.

Darn!

Well, it didn't matter now. I'd accomplished what I'd wanted, and I could tell Detective Jarvis exactly how the murder had taken place.

I hurried over to the glass door, unlocked it and slid it

open. "Officer Estavez," I began, but the woman who quickly slipped into the room was not Estavez. It was Stephanie Harmon, who was wearing the policewoman's jacket.

She pushed into the room, forcing me to back up. "Sorry I can't stay," I said, but I slammed into the dining-room table and bounced off it, landing in one of the side chairs.

Stephanie stood over me, a strange look on her face. "You shouldn't have been so nosy about the phone calls," she said.

I realized what that second click had been when I'd talked to Estavez. "You listened in, didn't you?"

She just smiled and moved closer. I tried to rise from the chair, but Stephanie planted herself directly in my way. It didn't take much imagination to know that I was in trouble and wasn't going to get out of this very easily.

But I tried. "Officer Estavez is going to come looking for her jacket," I told her.

Stephanie shook her head. "She doesn't even know it's missing, and as far as she's concerned, I'm sound asleep in my bedroom."

"That's what she thought Friday night, wasn't it? You heard Mrs. Duffy say the lock to this room was taped open, so you said you were going to rest, then unlocked the sliding glass door in your bedroom."

I paused, and she laughed. "So?" she asked. "What does that prove?"

I didn't like being laughed at, so angrily I snapped, "I'm not finished. You waited until Officer Estavez was in the bathroom. Then you sneaked out of your bedroom and left your suite through the door into the hallway. After you came into this suite and unlocked the glass door you called Frank Devane's room and asked him to meet you here. The operator remembered a woman calling from this suite."

"A woman? Is that all she told you?" Stephanie smiled again. "Then she didn't know who made the call."

Creepy fingers tickled up and down my backbone. I'd said too much. I knew that now. Why had I blabbed everything? I needed Detective Jarvis right this minute!

Once again I tried to rise, but Stephanie was on guard and shoved me back into the chair.

My big mouth had got me into this fix, but maybe it could help get me out. "You know they're going to discover everything," I said. "About the telephone call to your bank in the Cayman Islands, and—"

She gasped. "How did you learn about that?"

I would have enjoyed knowing that I had guessed right, but I was too frightened. "On the last day of the month people call their banks in Grand Cayman to find out the balances in their accounts," I said. "The phone number you called is in the hotel's computer records. It will be easy to learn the name of your bank."

Stephanie's forehead wrinkled, and I said, "When you screamed and yelled, 'He's after me!' it was pretty obvious that you knew Frank Devane. You weren't in danger because you were a witness in the trial. You were in danger because you'd been double-crossing Devane, and he'd found out before you got away with it. The money's in your Cayman Islands bank account, isn't it?"

"You have no proof that I killed him," she said.

"Because you didn't," I told her.

Stephanie was so surprised, she stepped backward, and that gave me my chance to shoot out of my chair and get the table between us. She circled, but I circled too. My back was to the glass door, but once I reached the other end of the table I could make a run for the door to the hallway. Once out there I could yell for Officer Estavez, and I hoped she'd hear me and come running.

Stephanie's eyes glittered, and she breathed quickly, panting a little. She was scared too. "You don't know who killed Frank," she said.

"I didn't until just a little while ago," I told her, "and then I figured it out. I'd heard Al Ransome say that he'd worked with Devane on everything, and it was obvious that Devane was no longer sure he could trust him. If you'd been cheating Devane, then you'd have been cheating Ransome, as well. But you weren't afraid of Ransome, the way you were with Devane, so I think the two of you worked together to double-cross Frank Devane, and when he began to discover what was happening, you decided to do away with him. You telephoned Al Ransome and told him how easy it would be. Then you invited Devane to come to this room, knowing you could sneak back to your own room and no one would even suspect you'd been here. Ransome committed the murder, but you're every bit as guilty, because you planned it."

Stephanie tried to sound haughty, but her voice wobbled. "Al and I have alibis," she said.

"You took the tape off the door so it would look as though the murderer had a key to the room. But you wanted the body to be found by the maid, who would come by for bed turn-downs around nine, so you propped the door ajar. If the door weren't open, she wouldn't have bothered with the room, because she knew no one was sleeping in it. You had a great alibi in Officer Estavez, who thought you were in your room asleep, and Ransome thought he was setting up an alibi by insisting he'd been in the bar since seven, but both alibis can be broken."

A familiar voice spoke behind me. "We'll have to get rid of her too," Al Ransome said.

The walls of the suite were probably pretty thick, and the sleuths wouldn't be on this floor until after they'd eaten, but hoping that Estavez . . . anyone . . . could hear me, at the top of my lungs I yelled, "Help! Somebody, help me!"

I honestly don't know what happened next. Later, Mrs. Duffy had me go over and over it, but that didn't help a bit. All I know is that the room exploded with a blast of music that could have been heard a block away. The big vase in the center of the table rose in the air, and I made a grab for it, but missed, and it came down on Al Ransome's head. Detective Jarvis burst through the hallway door at the same time, and he insisted he saw me swoop up that vase and clobber Ransome. But I couldn't have. I distinctly remember turning to run after Stephanie.

Officer Estavez, who'd been talking in the hallway with Detective Jarvis when the music nearly knocked them off their feet, came barreling into the room right behind him, and she said she saw me floor Stephanie with a right hook.

I wasn't even sure what a right hook was, but I wasn't going to argue with them or anyone else about what saved me. I just quietly whispered, "Thanks, Larry, for sticking around just a few minutes longer than you had to."

I think he heard me before he left. The others were too busy to notice the swirl and swoosh of cold air as it swept the room, then completely vanished.

Later, when Fran and I got together, I told him about Larry, and all Fran said was, "I wonder if he went to visit his wife in Digby."

That's what I liked so much about Fran. He was really a great guy, and even if he never grew tall enough to catch up with me, and even if my low self-esteem really was all mixed up in dating a short boyfriend, I decided I didn't care.

Down in the lobby Eileen took me aside and said, "Since you're officially one of our actors, you'll sit with us at the brunch tomorrow morning."

"Wow!" I said. "You mean I'll get real food?" But then I shook my head.

"We'll include Fran too," she said, misunderstanding my reason for hesitating.

"I'd better not come to the brunch," I insisted. "I told you, I'm pretty klutzy. What if I spill something and embarrass everybody?"

"Today at lunch I spilled my iced tea," she said.

"You?" I asked.

Eileen smiled. "Just between you and me, there was salad dressing on Sherlock Holmes's shirt, and one of the sleuths dropped her cheesecake into her lap. Everybody spills things."

"Low self-esteem," I said. "Tina explained it to me."

"Tina's wrong," Eileen said. She walked me over to a

mirror, holding my shoulders. "Take a good look at yourself."

"I'd rather not," I said. "Not on an empty stomach." But I sneaked a look anyway and saw Eileen's reflection. "I wish I looked like you," I said. "You're glamorous and poised and graceful, and you . . . well, you look as if you like yourself."

"That's the secret," Eileen said, "to like yourself the way you are. I've heard you saying you're klutzy and you're stupid. You keep insulting yourself. You wouldn't do that to a good friend, would you?"

"Of course not," I said.

"Then treat yourself just as nicely as you'd treat your good friend. Be a good friend to yourself. You'll find that when you learn to be at ease with yourself, the poise, the grace, and the charm follow."

"That won't help me look like you."

With both hands she swept up my hair and swirled it up and over the top of my head. I suddenly looked older and more sophisticated. "When I was your age," she said, "I had bangs and braces. But I learned to play with new hairstyles and makeup. You've got plenty of time ahead to try it too."

She let my hair drop, but I picked it up myself and held it this way and that. Maybe . . . just maybe she was right. I couldn't help feeling just a little bit excited.

Eileen said, "It's going to take time to develop your new self-image, Liz. Just promise me that you'll keep working on it."

"I will," I said, but I had another thought. "I've got a question about low self-esteem and a short boyfriend."

"No relation at all," Eileen answered. "Your boyfriend, for example. He's really a neat guy. He's got a lot more going for him than some of those tall hunks who are more interested in their own muscles than anything else."

I saw Fran charging across the lobby toward me, so I left Eileen and ran to meet him. In spite of the mystery-weekend people roaming around the lobby, I gave Fran a big hug.

"Is this part of the script?" he asked, hugging me back.

"No," I said.

"Then let's write our own," he suggested.

"With no murders in it," I said.

We started laughing, but Sherlock Holmes interrupted by tapping me on the shoulder.

"I want a straight answer," he said. "Did you have anything to do with the murder?"

"Whose?" I asked.

Sherlock rolled his eyes in exasperation. "What do you mean, whose? We've spent all weekend talking about Edgar Albert Pitts. Now, don't be evasive. Give me an answer."

I looked him right in the eyes and said, "I had nothing to do with his murder."

He studied me. "Of course, if you did, you wouldn't come out and say so. You'd lie. Are you lying?"

"No."

"How do I know that?"

"Because I told you."

"A murderer would lie."

"That's right, but I'm not a murderer."

He paused, never taking his eyes from mine. Finally, he shrugged and said, "You look honest, which probably means you aren't."

He walked away, but both Fran and I were questioned until close to the midnight deadline, when the teams who hadn't yet turned in their answer cards huddled together to come up with the solution, writing as fast as they could.

This had been one of the most exhausting days of my life, so I said good night to Fran and dragged myself up to my room, where I found the message light blinking insistently.

The operator told me that Mom wanted me to call, no matter how late, so I did.

As soon as I said "Mom," she interrupted.

"On the ten o'clock news they reported arresting the murderers of that savings-and-loan man. You just don't know how relieved I was to hear it."

"Me too," I said.

"Are you having fun, sweetheart?" she asked.

"A blast," I told her.

"I know the weekend's exciting, but are you sure you're getting enough sleep?"

"I'd be sleeping right now, Mom, except I got the message to call you."

"That's different," she said. "Tell me, are you eating well, dear?"

"Mom—"

"I mean, you're not just living on pizza are you?" she asked quickly.

"We don't get pizza around here. On a scale of one to ten, the employee cafeteria is a minus five," I said. I remembered what the morning would bring and felt a lot happier about the food situation. "Guess what, though. Tomorrow I get to eat brunch with the mystery-weekend group."

"Oh, lovely!" Mom said. "That should be fun." Her voice became more serious as she added, "Just remember, dear, that if the brunch is a buffet, there will be plenty of salad greens and fresh vegetables to choose from."

"And lots and lots of desserts," I added.

She didn't react, which was just as well. For some reason—maybe because of Eileen and what she said, or maybe because I'd helped solve the real murder and was feeling good about what I'd done—I said, "Mom, I wish you and Dad had been here. Some of the people who came to the mystery weekend are crazy, but they're all having an awfully good time. When I get home, I'll tell you all about it."

"I'll love that," Mom said. She suddenly gasped and added, "My goodness! Look at the time! You belong in bed, young lady. It's way past your bedtime!"

I said good night and grinned to myself. Life at the hotel was pretty exciting, but life at home hadn't changed a bit. Good old Mom.

The brunch was fantastic. There was so much food, I could only manage to eat three desserts. Everyone, except Fran and me, was excited and a little nervous, each team eager for the arrest to take place, so they'd know the winners. I did drop a buttered roll in my lap and began to say, "Oh, that was stupid of me," but I changed in mid-thought and—smiling at Mrs. Bandini, who was seated across from me—I said, "Thank goodness these rolls are light. I could have broken a leg."

Everyone close by laughed as though I'd made a great joke, and the man in the FBI sunglasses said, "She has a good sense of humor. She couldn't be the murderer."

I beamed at him, happy to note that a tiny bit of strawberry jam had slid down the front of his shirt.

Detective Sharp took the microphone and called the suspects up to the small stage at one end of the room. She went down the list, eliminating them one by one, while the teams cheered and clapped, or groaned because they'd made the wrong choice. When it came down to the last two, we all held our breaths. Then—surprise, surprise—the murderer turned out to be the desperate actress, Crystal Crane.

The members of Sherlock's team leaped to their feet, yelling and screeching and hugging each other. "I knew she did it!" Sherlock shouted.

The winners were awarded bottles of champagne, and Detective Sharp read a few of the entries. Except for Randolph, every other suspect had been guessed at least once. One team thought Detective Sharp committed the crime, and two of them guessed that I was the murderer.

"I was pretty sure it was you too," Fran murmured in my ear and squeezed my hand.

"It should have been the nephew," Mrs. Larabee muttered under her breath. "He's the only one of them who'll inherit, and now he'll get all Mr. Pitts's money, and I don't even like him—the nephew, that is."

All the actors were introduced, and I have to admit that I loved being the center of attention for even those few seconds. Remembering what Eileen had told me, I thought good, positive thoughts about myself and stood up as gracefully as I could, my head held high. Even though my chair fell over, no one seemed to notice or care.

When it was all over, Fran had to report for work, but I was free to go home. Well, not exactly free, because Mrs. Duffy latched on to me and said, "Mary Elizabeth, let's find a quiet place to talk. I want to hear all about the murder you solved when you began work at the Ridley in June."

We settled into a couple of chairs in one corner of the lobby, and she pulled out a small tape recorder, which surprised me.

"You're going to record what I say?"

"It will make it easier for me, if I decide to use your story in a mystery novel."

Tina had been right. If Mrs. Duffy wanted to write my story, then I'd be in a book! I'd be famous!

"Just tell me everything, in your own words, right from the beginning," Mrs. Duffy said, and turned on the recorder.

I closed my eyes, envisioning a drawing of myself on the book jacket. I'd be wearing my pink Ridley health-club T-shirt, and I'd be standing in front of the Ridley Hotel swimming pool, my long, red hair streaming around my shoulders. "How about this for a title," I said: "*The Dark and Deadly Pool*?"

HODDER

Another Hodder Children's book

THE DARK AND DEADLY POOL

Joan Lowery Nixon

Landing a summer job at the Ridley Hotel's glamorous health club is great at first, but as Mary Elizabeth makes her night-time rounds at the pool, where every sound echoes and the cold neon lights cast eerie shadows, she is uneasy.

Then one night, a ghastly shadow surges up from the pool and a terrified Mary Elizabeth confronts a face – eyes wide, mouth gaping – that slides beneath the surface of the pool and disappears.

Someone, or something, is watching Mary Elizabeth. Someone in the dark and deadly pool . . .

HODDER

Another Hodder Children's book

THE OTHER SIDE OF DARK

Joan Lowery Nixon

When Stacy McAdams wakes in a hospital room to discover she has been in a coma for the past four years, her problems are only just beginning.

An innocent thirteen-year-old trapped in the body of a mature seventeen-year-old, Stacy had a lot of catching up to do. She yearns for the familiarity of her previous world.

Stacy is heartbroken to discover that her mother has been killed. Murdered by the same stranger who shot Stacy four years ago – and she is the only eye-witness. The only eye-witness to a murderer who hasn't yet been caught . . .

WHEN DARKNESS COMES

Robert Swindells

'Everybody thinks that Daf will be our next chief. But Daf is grown gentle with age – he supports the old chief, who is too feeble to lead us. Soon both will be swept away. Then *we shall see who brings who to the earth!'*

So threatens Gyre to his rival Morg at the start of a conflict ridden with jealousy and ambition that will split their whole community . . .

THE GHOST MESSENGERS

Robert Swindells

Haunted by the ghosts of her grand-father and his wartime bomber crew, Meg tries to make sense of their strange and puzzling messages. These super-natural experiences disturb her sleep and her schoolwork and seem somehow intensified by the conservation work in local woodland. As the warnings build to a climax, can Meg decipher the message before it's too late?